WHERE EBON SOUNDS LIKE IVORY

The second of the Norn Novellas

A. NICKY HJORT

First Edition

The Norn Novella Series book 2

2017 Lavish Publishing, LLC

All Rights Reserved

Published in the United States by Lavish Publishing, LLC, Midland, TX

Cover Design by: WYCKED INK

Cover Images: ADOBE STOCK

Paperback Edition

ISBN: 9781944985448

www.LavishPublishing.com

Contents

For Kimberly, my baby sister,
who has the most important job in the world on Christmas morn—
keeping everyone's feet warm while they open the gifts that Santa delivers.

Acknowledgments

Acknowledgments and Comments:

If you know me well, you know that I really do, honestly, not kidding, mean it for reals—without crossed fingers—believe in Santa Claus. His spirit is so very palpable to me, and although you may doubt my sincerity, I am not jesting in the least. Yet as a reader of the kinds of books I tend to write, maybe that is also true for you. Oh…I hope; I do. Should you ever find yourself doubting Father Christmas, I hope you'll be pleased to know that each year he finds a new way to prove himself to me even though.

I was raised with a faith that didn't allow me to celebrate Christmas nor believe in the man with a big, white beard. These days, for the heck of it, I celebrate Christmas all year long to catch up from childhood. I mean, a girl has to do what a girl has to do, don't you think? I suggest you believe in him too. Not say you do, but mean it…like you mean you love the sight of freshly fallen snow or the way the ocean teases as it pushes and pulls on the shoreline forever. Like that. Then I suppose his gifts—in the most delightful and unexplainable ways—will find you too. Remember, like the great Roald Dahl said, "Those who don't believe in magic will never find it."

Usually Santa's small treasures present themselves to me and mine in the most surprising of ways as inexpensive yet profoundly symbolic gifts that cannot come from anyone but Santa. The wintry Father who knows all of me whether I believe in him or not...like Odin knows Za...in the deepest and most highly guarded corners of my mind and heart.

Of note, also...should you feel compelled to check, you will find that many modern Christmas traditions are in fact rooted in Norse Mythology. Thus, it is no accident that Za should appear in this of all stories. And that I, of all people, should be the one to tell it.

Also of note, this fairytale is based on an alternate realm and the terrible beings and horrific creatures first described by...my late father, James William Hjort, in a short story he called *The Ebon Harp*. It was first, and only to this date, published in his anthology, *Ebon Roses, Jewelled Skulls*. The rights to which were passed to me.

My father died three years ago...almost to the day that I finish this Novella.

Jim Hjort's stories, should you read them, are all dark, disturbing, and end in the most gruesome of ways. He wanted to change that after finding the forgiveness of his Maker, finally at peace with the demons that had tormented and haunted him his whole life. His last request of me was that I reinvent, re-layer, and recreate his stories to give his characters a more likable nature. This is my first attempt at honoring said request. So on my father's behalf, I wish you all a very merry Christmas, a surprising gift you cannot and will not ever be able to explain without magic, the warmest of toes, and as always...the happiest of endings. Or beginnings. Or middles. Or anywhere in between.

As for the three people without whom this story could have never existed, this time, and only this time …there is but one. The most charming Prince, who one day, just like in Snow's beautiful song, did finally come. Only this life, unlike her, I plan to walk with him in the living and not in the dying.

Back to Za then… She has a story about a harp, Father Christmas, and the proper origins of a classic fairytale to share. Are you ready?

ONE

Legend of the Ebon Harp

Play the Ebon Harp with fingers light…
Wait, dare not to touch, lest you might,
Bring such demons forth…this Solstice night.
Unless…unless…
Your blood-red kisses of life, do trade,
Otherworldly passion of love's fairest maid,
And you're the only creature who ever stayed.
Safely abreast the devil's malicious shore…
And by helping Snow be as black as noir,
Forever closed an un-closable door.

TWO

The Ebon Harp

ZA, the hardly known yet most intriguing of the four immortal Norn Sisters, left her bed early before the sunrise on the verge of winter's Solstice. If she had real, living parents to speak of, the curious creature would most likely have run to them for advice yet again, but alas…the only limited guidance offered her during crisis came from her adopted father figure, Odin, ruler of her universe.

And as usual around the time of winter's Solstice, he was always too busy creating this or destroying that or whatever it was he was always doing. Of course, like the commoners in her homeland, she could simply hang her request for the Solstice Saints. Saints…probably elves or dwarves, more like, whom she had long suspected were some collection of Odin's lesser minions in ridiculous costumes, from the large and vibrant Yggdrasil World Tree in the center of the village. There the villagers hung their prayers and most heart-felt wishes by a string, made of their most precious scrap materials, from the reachable branches of the mysterious tree—a huge plant that always managed to be as green as freshly slimed frog skin.

Well, always except for the branch of the dead and damned, of course.

Za had stood at the base of the massive plant, three meters wide at least, on many of occasions trying to figure out what sort of spell made it grow and grow despite the deepest chills of winter and the driest of summers. Seasons when Frey, the god of rain and sun, had surely forgotten that precious water from the sky was as critical as warmth from the sun to bless the people that kept multiplying under his fertile guardianship. Where at that lone woody vision that dwarfed Za, as tall and mighty as the doors of Odin's legendary hall in Asgard were wide, it was whispered that Solstice Saint do-gooders might come to collect the villager's greatest wishes the days and nights that came before the Solstice. *Might. Might. Might.*

But *might* had never been good enough for a thing as feisty as Za. And surely Odin's own adopted, immortal *daughter* deserved to be treated better than common town folk with such broken and rarely answered half-promises like *might*. Ridiculous bargains by such unimportant imposters who pretended to be things they could never be. Only Odin himself was worthy of filling that role. And if anyone knew Odin couldn't be bothered to fulfill his promises, it was she. What a lazy god he was, she thought. What had he ever suffered for his lowly people? She wasn't sure why they dropped to their knees to sing and praise such a sloth of a ruler. Odin never bothered anything about her, and she was immortal herself even though he—the supposedly highest and mightiest amongst them—wasn't. How could he possibly be bothered to deliver up wishes to help mere, unworthy humans who worshiped beneath his one great eye and trembled at his stinky feet?

Besides, she didn't believe in legends she herself had not invented until she saw them firsthand. Never had, never would. That was simply her nature.

Thus, the clever, but devastated, black-haired beauty sought solace in the only thing she knew was real for sure—magic. Magic of her own. Magic that came from whatever had blessed, or possibly even cursed, her mother at birth. A common mortal's birth that had somehow, according to what little was known of the event, resulted in the delivery of four girls. All of them born exactly one hour apart before their mother succumbed to her weakness—mortality—finding solace in the god Hel's arms of eternal sleep. The same kind of peace that Za had never felt as a result of losing the irreplaceable, a proper childhood, before she even knew what she had lost.

It had been several nights since Za had found the device, that enrapturing ebon masterpiece divinely carved with the most interesting designs, tucked away in some corner of her birth family's tomb that she had never explored before. It was a long story why she had come to be there and find it, but she couldn't be bothered to think about that right now. Besides, she didn't dare think about the consequences of what had happened last night and what it could mean. She had one night, two at most, to fix things, or the curse would last for all eternity.

She looked at the two items in her hand and stashed them away while nervousness ate her from the inside like the wormy parasites that chew on the deepest branches of the World Tree to stave off their hour of inevitable demise. A ribbon. A hair comb. How could two items, so simple and plain, cause so much bother? Maybe it was a lie. Maybe it wasn't. How would she ever know?

"Thank Odin the payments can be paid later. I just don't have the time or the tyme before winter Solstice." Toying with the possibility of re-creating tyme, a world where she had learned that the hell-of-Tyndra and the heaven-of-Ardnyt were the exact same places just moving in different directions, she felt better. She always found a way to escape the punishment for her selfish crimes. This time would be no different. What did she care if she didn't have His Majesty's full attention? She had her sorcery, and she could create worlds all on her own, especially with the help of an enchanted harp. Maybe she would forsake her promise to the woman and never return.

She could play the harp all on her own, could she not?

"What a lovely waste of tyme," she whispered and winked to her friend, a fox she loved with all her heart. But Talby was getting on in age, as foxes tend to do, and wouldn't be around much longer. That gave her an idea. She cracked her knuckles.

Everyone knows a saucy Norn sister with an idea could be quite a dangerous thing. But what things in life that were not dangerous had ever been truly fun? Could the harp really grant her most secret wish...for such a small price—unlike Father Odin...who was so busy playing the grand host to the heroes in his grand hall in Asgard that he had totally forgotten about her?

She had to find out what the player of an ancient harp could do with such simple things, why they were so important. And why the barmaid, who any fool could see was a used-up old witch in disguise standing precariously at the edge of death herself already, wanted to play it so badly. Did she think she could stave off damnation and the passage across the Ebon Branch of the Dead? Surely not. Even witches met their maker's judgment at the end of their days of evildoing.

Mind made up, Za stood and straightened her back fine and strong and decided to play it another time...just to get answers. So many questions required so many answers. Quickly, she braided her long, black hair and tucked it up into a bun so that it would stay in place. She gathered her bo staff and puffed her chest out to augment the courage the wooden stick instilled in her.

"You stay here, Talby. You put out the shoes like I promised Doc I would to collect the wishes that no one ever brings." A tear threatened, but she managed to pull it back in before it fell. "And I'll be back by the fire before Solstice morn to fill them myself like every year before because we all know that Solstice Saints are not real." She petted her feathery friend and started walking away with a small and worn book in her pocket.

She had a harp to play, after all.

An ebon harp, to be exact…

THREE

The Sixth Day and the Sixth Playing of the Harp—Part One

HALFWAY TO THE hidden spot of her treasure, Za stopped to snack and rest and think once more. The small book in her pocket felt heavier by the moment. Perhaps it was time to take it out and read it then. She remembered the words of the witch from last night. "You're not much of a reader, surely…are you, dear?" And the way the old hag, disguised as a young barmaid, kept staring at her bar glasses and avoiding eye contact.

"No, not much. That's true," Za had replied. But when she saw the satisfied glance go across the old woman's face looking up a bit too hopeful, she decided finding that old book might not be the worst idea she had ever had. And even the pointy-eared elves of Alf Heim, always looking for ways to ignore the laws of Midgard or Earth, knew that was saying something.

"Good. That's good," the wretch had added, and Za was immediately reminded of a few of the stories she liked to whisper in the ears of those terribly stupid, but getting more famous by the day, brothers Grimm. Stories about beasts and sleeping beauties and the like. Most of the absurdly boring and stupid princesses tricked by an old witch before a prince or a kiss (even more absurd) saved them. *Good? Not good.*

"But I like a nice story," Za told the old woman. "In fact, I am always on the lookout for the next tale. Where are you from anyway?"

"Gnopt."

"Funny, Gnopt funny," Za teased but thought better of it when she felt the evil eyes of the woman bore into her soul. "I mean, funny. I've never heard of Gnopt."

"Ah, that might be true, child with such a lonely heart, but we in Gnopt have heard of you. You are…how shall we say…quite infamous for what happened with the releasing of the Enfield creature."

"He was not a creature. He was a—"

"Never mind about old monsters and their Ivy Walls. All forgotten. You didn't mean… Well, all forgiven anyway, dear."

Forgiven? What?

"And don't you, you sweet thing, go believing old legends about raising the dead too much either. The ebon…"—and here the creep coughed; that much Za remembered for sure—"…that was not about any harp you might find. That must be a sister replica, one that never belonged to the Darkest Master or was affected by such…how shall we say…side effects. Never. Nope, not that one. That one is as safe as a garden snake or a little old velvet worm."

"Don't you people in Gnopt know that velvet worms are actually voracious, nocturnal predators that eat small arthropods and invertebrates by ensnaring them in slime and then biting a hole into their victims and sucking out the soft insides?"

"Brilliant. I mean, terrible. And I said earthworms, not velvet worms."

"No, you didn't."

Side effects? Sister harp? Za knew a few things about side effects and siblings. And darkness, for a matter of fact. Perhaps she would find the book the old witch had hinted about…just to be sure.

A day's worth of hunting in every musty old library, when she should have been out building snowmen or hanging lights, to find it—the last copy of *Ebon Roses, Jewelled Skulls* by an old wizard from the outskirts of Zobarth known simply as Sir James. She was sworn to secrecy and had to hand over one of two pieces of her finest gold coins to get the name of someone who *might* possibly have a name of someone who *might* possibly know where it was. But it was fiction, not to be taken seriously, not to be believed as real, or it *might* scare her too much.

Za had two thoughts about that:

One, what a hefty price for so many *mights.* Maybe the tree back in town was the best way to get what she wanted after all? But definitely not as much fun, she realized, and her mind was made up to not only read the story but to play the harp herself again.

And two, if the world of Tyndra had taught her anything, it was that the deepest, most highly guarded secret of those who weave tales is—a story is never just a story. None of them ever are. Or ever have been.

In the slightest light of the barely rising sun behind her, she turned to the proper chapter of the book, *The Ebon Harp,* and marked the page with a crimson ribbon she pulled from her pocket as she approached her birth family's tomb. The other item in her trousers—a small, fragile, red and white swirled alabaster comb—she pushed into her hair to hold back the loose strands that had fallen out of her braid.

"There, hair. Stay safely put." *Not safely put.* The sensation of worms sliming through her guts returned like a morbid warning of what lies deep beneath the soil in the darkest, dark places no one dare speak of in proper company.

Other than her and her three sisters, all of the family from whence she came had been declared dead and crumbling to ash in this tomb. Although, after a conversation she had overheard in the local tavern, she had explored the lavish graves. With indescribable pain at the implication of the meaning of it, she found them naught but headstones above or beside ornate yet so disappointingly empty caskets.

Her family, specifically her mother, had not died; she had left—obviously. Like a satisfied spider perhaps leaves her mate after consuming his head to go and gestate his orphaned children. She wondered, in this case, who had eaten whom and if the web of an arachnid was any different than the slime of a velvet worm.

Such different yet similarly effective bloodsucking techniques.

No one knew about the empty graves save her and the local physician. Well, and the old couple in the tavern, of course— the aged pair just within in her earshot, heads down, eyes shrouded in cloaks and speaking a language that was close enough to her native tongue for her to understand bits and pieces.

She brought her thoughts back to her immediate environment and approached the massive black gate surrounding Crypt De' Norn. It was hard to tell for sure, but best her eyes could calculate, the span of the grave was about twice as wide across as it was deep. Probably fifty meters give or take. And the entire thing was enclosed in an onyx, wrought iron fence with razor-sharp tips as formidable to an intruder trying to steal some possibly hidden treasures as the red, glowing fire in the rainbow bridge was treacherous to the icy feet of frost giants and trolls.

The crypt, as usual, made her take pause to remember that she couldn't die. She and her sisters were the only ones. Even

Odin and his powerful sons were subject to death. But not she. Why, she wondered. How, she wondered.

As an immortal, there were no ends of days left decomposing as bone turned to dust for Za. Only lessons inside never-ending lessons, each more difficult to pass than the last. Until… the darkness in her soul was so light and small and impossible that her feet could ascend enough on the branches of the Odin's Tree to see for herself if Gimlé, the highest heavens above Asgard, was just another false threat of the All-Father to keep the lesser gods in place. Until then, she would have to take *His Word*, which was hardly much more than silence.

A raven, familiar to her by this point in our story, cawed far off in the distance, and chills coursed through her body. Yet Za unlocked the creaking, heavy metal gate anyway. She marched the ten paces forward, paused, and placed her right hand in the crimson and silver water bowl made of marble as thick as her wrist that guarded the entry. The bracelet flashed. Then as usual, the small amount of cold water contained therein gathered speed, staining her hand along with her golden bracelet—a token from Odin. The fluid seemed to heat up and multiply in amount with the gift only a magical creature like she had, filling a red bowl with an even deeper red liquid.

"What a waste of my power, All-Father," she said and blew air out her pursed lips. But she couldn't help but wonder if it was her hand or the bracelet, the same perdurable one all of her other sisters also were forced to wear by Odin's law, that activated the bizarre spell.

None Potest Intrare Norns, inscribed in Latin above the marble bowl, quickly turned into her native tongue—*Only Norns May Enter*—as her hand sank deeper and deeper into the flowing bloodstained water from nowhere. The two massive concrete columns of the crypt opened wide, allowing the doors to retreat inside themselves as the water in the bowl disappeared into the few drops that birthed the previous buckets of swimming red liquid. She shook her hand, now back to its normal color, and repeated her words. "What a waste of my power, All-Father."

As she stepped forward, several bats flew past, and the chills and wormy guts returned. She gripped the book in her left hand even tighter and attempted to drain her swirling thoughts magically, just like the bowl, by shaking her bracelet back and forth. But it was no use. The thoughts just gathered speed instead. So as usual, she ignored her turbid thoughts and smiled in surrender to the fact that she always did what she wanted to even when her stomach argued with her mind.

Now...if Za was the kind of girl who listened to her inner voice and admitted her very reasonable fears, this is where she would have, and most certainly should have, run back home. But Za, as even the one-eyed Odin and almost always-silent god would have told you, was not, and had never been, the same as other girls. It has oft been said that girls are made of sugar, spice, and all things nice. Za, in contrast, was more likely made of cinnamon, spite, and all things fight. There was a reason Odin had given her the infinite assignment of wasting time. It was to keep her out of trouble. Yet, as was often the case, even the best-laid plans of one as powerful as the All-Father did not turn out the way they were expected to.

It is here that our adventure really begins. On one of the final nights she plans to move and then play the harp. On the night she reads the book about the last time the harp played for its previous master under such...circumstances. Once Za opens the ancient manuscript written by Sir James, she cannot go back in time, no matter how many alternate or parallel realities she creates, and not see what is actually written there in *Ebon Roses, Jewelled Skulls*—a powerful collection of tales about the darkest demons from the most terrible realms hidden deep behind, between, and underneath the beauty of her new world. Old stories from before the word story was thought of, disguised as fiction that are not, nor have ever been, just stories. Nightmares that play out for fools stupid enough to delve deep into such matters because such things were birthed from within a pit of dark energy that existed long before the graceful concept of light. Stories that could not be more contrasted by beautiful myths and fables about gods with unselfish intentions, or Fates with threads to weave, or bridges made of rainbows to save those that cutting of such golden strings had destined to souls to travel next along the dead or Ebon Branch of the World Tree.

FOUR

The Sixth Day Continued–Za Opens the Collected Written Works of Sir James

THE LINEN PAGES of the text seemed to Za to be as heavy as boulders to turn. Parchments possibly even soaked with uncontainable suffering that oozed from its author onto her fingers as she simply touched the pages he had once touched. The opening words of his—sections marked with page numbers, inscribed with ink made of misery and old blood—now became her words and drank of her blood as she read them out loud.

"Dragonride. Cthulhu's Gold. Conclusion of the Griffin's Game. Dust of the Necro…romancer. The Ebon Harp."

She stopped there. "The Ebon Harp. Page forty-one." But she didn't finish the rest of the names and places, some so old they were thought to have come into the world before the first gods and giants. Back when Norse legend told that there was no earth, no sun, no moon, no stars…only Niflheim, a waste of frozen fog above, and Muselheim, a place of eternal fire below. But in between these two realms, for untold ages that existed before the concept of time or light, there was a gaping pit of dismal and dark energy.

She quickly scrolled down the rest of the list. Here she thought but dared not speak the words because she feared their mere utterance might bring them back to life with her attention to them. *Andalous. Chimera. Garden in the Shadows. Dead Yothin. Valley of the Dead. The Orb of Xom...*

Even the thought of Xom-Orhon was too painful to complete, and she quickly turned the first page to see the picture of a dragon-giant, a terrible creature that even the jotuns, now commonly known as frost giants, in the far away mountains cowered from. She slammed the book shut. But not before Sir James's words contaminated her. His darkness now spread into her mouth, her eyes, and became hers through the guilt of association. But inner darkness, no matter how deep, had yet to really scare her away long enough to win her internal inner battle between what was made from good and innocence in Odin's eyes and what was interesting to her adventurous and wild nature. This time would be no different.

She turned the manuscript over and trailed her finger down the crumbling spine. Was she this brave?

"Or am I this stupid?" she asked, and a raven outside cawed. "I'll take that as a yes," she said and laughed just enough to feel better about what she was about to do.

Quickly, she opened the book once more, careful to avoid so much as thinking about the words that mentioned the places where the dark and dismal pit was rumored to still linger in drops. Places with remnants of evil drizzle that should never be named despite all the work of the first Aesir Gods of the Norse, including Odin. Back before the goodness of Earth or the World Tree was created. Back when the six original gods slew Ymir, the largest and meanest of the first frost giants, and pushed his horrible, huge hulk into the pit. They did this, her childhood stories told her, both to kill the awful cannibalistic monster named Ymir and fill the swirling dark energy with something large and terrible enough to envelop and absorb it. Obviously, they missed a few drops.

Za took a breath to quiet her mind. One, two, three breaths.

"Oh, shut up and piss off," she told herself, which worked better than the breathing or shaking her hand. "There. That's better."

The reflection from her mother's small but undeniably beautiful mirror, the one that hung above the grave marked with a series of runes, accused her of doing things she shouldn't do but had to.

"I said that's better, didn't I?" she claimed, but the worms had buried too deep inside her bowels to ignore them. "Fine. I'll just feel nervous. I don't care."

About the size of a hairbrush, with an oddly ethereal nature to the smoky-white edges of the glass itself held in place by a rim of golden carvings as wide as her thumb, the mirror could only be described as *otherworldly*. It felt to her, while she looked into it, that Za could both fall into it and out from it at the same time. Getting more lightheaded the longer she stared at her own profile in the oval work of undeniably perfect crafts- manship, Za appeared forlorn and haunted. Another three breaths and a few more curses at the chill in the air didn't help.

Her image looked more like the legends, now that she knew them, of her famously beautiful mother than herself. The same mother with a forbidden name, Nevis, whom Za had never actually met…in person. The one with piercing, yet sad, charcoal grey eyes…except for a small sparkle of green at the edges that was rumored to be the source of her once- revered power to ensnare even the most loyal man to do her bidding. Her eyes so alluring, her hair so captivating, it was rumored that Za's mother was the object of every village man's and even a few god's affections. Never once had she ever lacked for attention with her full, blood-red pouted lips to contrast the pale, but as smooth as a crystal ball, skin. Shiny, black hair, straight as a pencil but as thick as a broomstick's handle, that hung to her mid back over her narrow shoulders and high and well-breasted chest. The woman had been described by many as a tortured child trapped in the body of a hungry siren who must have consumed her own youth in anger for unknown, probably unspeakable crimes. Everyone wanted her. No one possessed her. No one knew what had really happened to her.

And Odin, that grump, refused to tell Za any more than he told her older sisters about the cause of their mother's untimely passing.

Unable to resist and hoping to lighten her mood and rumbling tummy, she spoke to the thing. "Mirror, my mirror, from mother's gravesite, send me"—she paused here thinking of something clever to say—"your desperate daughter, a bit of light."

And to Za's surprise, the tomb became just a wee bit brighter despite the closing of the outer doors.

And just as she expected, she heard the caw of the raven she had come to consider an odd friend, from somewhere both left and right and forward and backward. A familiar beast, who although she should consider it a bad omen to see, she had noticed seemed to always show up at the right time this past week like he was a result of some unseen master's gifts of synchronicity.

So she asked again for more light. And once more, the vault seemed a little bit brighter, almost bright enough to read by. The third time she asked, her wish was adequately granted.

"That is a mirror, Mother, that unlike you, I think I shall keep as long as I shall live," she said to a few squeaking mice looking for scraps of food they would never find. A snake slithered from the corner, and she considered that the vermin rodents were more likely to become food than to find it in a place like this.

"Sorry, not sorry, little mousy," she hissed, mocking the snake and laughing.

Feeling much less afraid than she should have considering the type of material in her hand, she opened the ancient book once more. The smell of ages long since forgotten, laced with a faint slice of old blood, filled her nostrils. She coughed and cleared her throat. Then she quickly flipped to page forty-one of the disintegrating pages, trying harder than she dared to admit not to read any of the others.

"I sit alone in a darkened room and stare at the harp...the ebon, sorcerer-engraved harp. It sits at arm's length from me, so close that I might reach out and touch its delicately wrought surface, feel the interplay of its carven shapes and forms, feel the glyphs of some demon melody.

"I write this now, for I know not what may befall me when the harp is played for the seventh time. Regardless of the outcome, this record in ink and parchment shall survive me and stand as a witness to the events having transpired these past few days."

She looked at her hands and almost dropped the book at the coincidence.

Seven. She was about to play it for the sixth time. Wow.

Thankfully, she hadn't let it fall away, because surely the withered pages would have disappeared into total nothingness from the impact.

"The seventh time? Seriously? Tell me more, my little book," she said, her voice almost shaking as she stretched out her legs to get comfortable before reading more. She snapped her fingers, and with two more words, the room became bright enough for any young creature like her to read just fine by. "Mirror, lighter."

"Now as it stood in the chamber, capturing my attention as would the sight of an enchantress, I stepped forward to examine

its surface, touching its intricately engraven shapes and symbols, some recognizable, others as foreign to me as the writing of dead civilizations and long-perished scribes. And as lightly as one stroking the soft fur of some black cat"—or my fox, Talby, Za thought—"*I trailed my fingers along the strings, setting the air astir with a flowing cascade of musical notes —notes which poured crisply and ambrosially forth from the harp."*

She stood and approached the harp before she continued.

"Not having been so close to a harp before, I found myself amazed at the melodious tones produced by this single stroke. For there seemed to be such a harmonious blending of sounds, such beauteous tones, that I was intensely pleased with myself and even fancied someday mastering the instrument."

She grudgingly whispered the following words, holding on to them too tightly like precious jewels stolen from her lips. "Such was the first time I played upon the harp." She sighed remembering that fateful day and sank into the recollection of it. "That, dear James of Zobarth. Me, too." And she trembled, fingers poised to strum the strings as she descended upon the memory of the day.

FIVE

Day One: The First Playing of the Harp

AS WAS her routine on Friday evenings, Za went around to the local tavern to listen to the never-ending stories of old told by the aged women and men who had no one left still willing to hear them. Some widowed too soon by the cruel plans of fate, others just too fond of holding their drinks to hold on to their husbands or wives, the regulars at the Dvergr's Tavern had become a family of their own by default...that no one seemed to love but her.

She stood at the door and listened before she entered. Here they were, as always on Friday night, telling the same old stories about the same old things no one cared about anymore. She peeked through the door and giggled at the four of them still there after dinnertime. Austri—the comedian who made fun of everything. Vestri—an old grump of a man who was pissed off by everything. Norori—always tired, who would always rather be in bed. And Suori—an aging physician who had more heart than hair left on his bald head.

"Austri, I'd sure like to see all the diamonds you are always bragging about...because your debt here has gotten even larger than your fishing stories, you old goose," the barkeep, Vestri, hollered from across the small, poorly lit room.

"I'll show my bigg...est diamond of 'em all," Austri, an unusually short statured but well-bearded bachelor yelled more toward the door than the bar because his sense of direction had disappeared along with his last drink. "Because" —he paused trying to remember his next words—"we all...lll know my cock-a-doodle-doo isss wayyy big...ga...ger than yoursssss." He laughed, certain he had just said the funniest thing ever. Then as the silliest of the four, he felt obliged to stand up both to dance a jig and show the fellows his grey hair-covered tender bits, a favorite trick of his. But gravity and all the drinks got the best of him, and he fell down face first, balls still cupped tightly, instead.

Vestri, both the owner of the place—one that had been handed down from father to son for too many generations to count—and its most loyal patron, stood up to help his best friend. But he forgot where he was going and sat back down on his stool and wobbled back and forth. He tried to speak but just hiccuped.

From the floor, Austri said, "Diamonds. Mine's the biggest rooster of 'em all." Still he clenched his tenders, oblivious to the expanding lump on his forehead.

"What? That makes no sense," the classically most bitter and drunk amongst the men, Vestri, replied. "What was I doing?" he asked and wobbled a bit more.

"My rooster makes perfect sense to me. Ha!"

"Rooster. What? Oh, you mean cock, not rooster, you idiot."

"That's what I said. Cock. Diamond. Real prize here."

"Whatever, old man. That's why you're here with us every night instead of dancing under the covers of your bare bed with a juicy but ugly maiden from the icy mountains."

"Ohhh, that's cold." Austri giggled and rolled over on his back, eyes closed.

"Very punny," Vestri said and deepened the scowl on his always-furrowed brow.

"Thanks, old man. Dang, I almost forgot. I have a new joke. Hey guys, what did the elephant say to the naked sailor?"

"Oh no, here he goes with another…rooster joke," Norori said from the farthest booth, yawning. "Do not laugh. Whatever you do, do not laugh. His happy ass will never stop telling lame jokes, and I will never get to bed. Again. Oh fut-a-stick."

Of course, they all laughed because Norori would never say the real f-word and used "fut" in its place…as if that was somehow more innocent. And much to Norori's dismay, who was always trying to get home to bed but never seemed to manage to accomplish it when a pitcher of mead was involved, the whole placed roared.

He scratched his sleepy eyes and laid his head on the table. "Tired and dizzy. Bad combo. Oh, fut-a-duck. I'm screwed."

"Hey, not screwed, never screwed, actually, you unlucky bastard, " Austri continued, feeling strong enough to push his head off the floor for a moment and giggle. "He said, 'that's cute and all, but can you breathe through it?'"

"What?" Norori, the sleepy one, asked. "Breathe through what?"

"The elephant. Breathe through it. Get it?" the fat, happy comedian replied.

"What the fut are you talking about?" Norori asked, slamming his foot on the floor, probably more to slow the spinners than for effect.

"The elephant, his trunk. The sailor's rooster. My joke, you drunk, old fool. Pay attention," Austri said and lay back down, moaning in between laughs.

"It's a cock, Mister Happy Pants. Not a rooster."

"Yes, that's what I said, Mister Grumpy Face." Austri laughed even louder.

"No, you didn't," Vestri said and wobbled some more.

"Funny, not a bit futting funny," Norori said in his thick accent, banging his foot on the floor and head on the table in perfect timing while he yawned again.

"Fut if it isn't, Mister Sleepy Ass," Austri muttered, imitating his friend's accent perfectly and making everyone laugh more at Norori than the elephant joke.

"Nice impression, Happy," Za said and opened the wooden door.

Vestri steadied himself enough to make eye contact with her and wave her inside. Talby, her fox, wasn't far behind. After barking and snarling to let the men know he would protect her at all costs, the adorable creature went and sat by the dwindling fire.

"What was I doing?" the tavern owner asked again and hiccuped.

"Probably," Za replied, "going to help your best fr-enemy up off the floor, Vestri." She stood over Austri, still hardly breathing because he was laughing so hard about his silly joke. "That goose egg," Za said, "is going to sting tomorrow no matter how many jokes you tell."

The comedian let go of his privates and checked the bump. "Oh. Ouch."

She leaned over the old comedian to examine the lump on his forehead. "Yep. Ouch. Bad one."

"Oh, yes. Help Austri. That was it." Vestri tried to stand but still couldn't.

"I've got him. Sit down before I have to pick you up too," Za said.

"Doctor Suori, some help please. Norori, ice for the newly born unicorn here before you fall asleep back there, please.

Vestri, drink some coffee, and then when you can stand without causing me more bother, help me put the kettle on, and rekindle that joke of a fire."

Vestri hiccuped once more but managed to stand. "Do you think it is a coincidence or a cruel joke from his mother, who was an even worse comedian than he, that Austri's name is almost Ass-tree?"

The others laughed at the statement because Vestri, that grumbling old boot, meant what he had just said and was not trying to be funny at all.

"On that note, the bar is officially closed, my favorite four old dudes. Where are your other three pals?" Za said.

"Don't worry," Vestri said. "They are busy plotting and planning somewhere else. Okay. You're right. Dvergr's Bar is closed. Besides, we are totally out of booze and cookies."

Za looked up at the sign above the bar. "Vestri, what does Dvergr's mean? Was that a family name?"

"No," he replied. "It means 'dwarf' in the old, old language."

"Hmm, didn't know that." And as usual, she methodically went about the business of sobering them up, sweeping out the small room, and getting them safely home one by one before the deepest chill of the night took hold.

Suori, an old, retired physician, both the kindest and oldest of the crew, helped her walk the other three home. And after a nice cup of ginger tea and locking up the bar, he allowed her to walk him home last. Normally, he would have refused, but he loved Za's company so much he didn't have the fortitude to decline her offer to hear one more of his doctor stories along the way back home.

Almost to his small but tidy quarters, they passed rather close to the Norn crypt, and he paused, deep in thought, before turning down the path to his house. "Let me tell you a story I have never told you," he said and bit his lip.

She smiled despite her tired feet and the late hour.

"Actually, I have never told anyone. Why I live here, so close to the graves."

"We all assumed you miss your old patients," Za said and laughed.

"Oh, Za, I don't miss them anymore than I missed seeing Austri's balls again tonight. His hairy rooster neck could use a trimming." They both laughed.

"Go on then," she said and winked.

"This one is about her. About Snow." He tilted his head toward the tomb.

"Snow? My mother? Oh, I almost forgot you must have been the village physician when she...when I was born. When she...left."

He sighed.

"Good Doctor, did you care for her when…"

"No. Oh no. You misunderstand. I wasn't allowed in the delivery room that night. I didn't take care of her. But I would have. I mean, I would have done anything for her. I loved her."

"You loved her?"

"Very much. Didn't you know?"

"I didn't realize"—she sat down on the front porch—"you even knew my mother. Why…? But how…? You never… Are… Are you my father?"

"Oh, no. We never… I never… No. No, I wish." He sat down beside her and patted Za's knee. "Oh, my sweet child, we all knew your mother."

"But—"

Talby barked, making sure they remembered he was there too.

"Oh, we haven't forgotten you," the old man said and leaned over to pet the animal. "I wanted her to be my bride. Had asked for her hand, but…but…" He licked his lips and slowly added, "She was…was stolen from me."

"Stolen?"

"Stolen," he said and swallowed so hard Za heard his jaw click.

"What? How? Why have you never said…?"

He massaged the back of his neck and took a few deep breaths. "Come in, and I'll tell you all about it even though some stories are best left…untold. It is time, I think, for you to hear this one." He took her into the main room and gathered a few furs to wrap her in and gave the fox some scraps of dried beef.

"Yes. Tell me."

"Nevis, God forgive me…" He coughed and bowed his head while wringing his hands. "Her name, Nevis…it means 'snow' in the old language. Not snow like the deadly ice that blows from the evil jowls of the jotun frost giants but pure, untainted snow that falls on winter Solstice as a gift from the highest clouds above Asgard."

"I didn't realize that."

"Yes, your mother was a sight of purity for many a sore eye who immediately loved her. We all loved her. In fact, her unearthly smooth, creamy skin and old, sad eyes were the subject of many poems and songs when we were young. Bragi still sings a few of them. And her name became a legend. So much so that a dreadful ogress took notice and grew wild with envy. But your mother—"

"An ogress? Wait. You mean that bitch, Angerboda?"

"Yes, her." The retired doctor clenched his fists.

"Wasn't she…?"

"Yes. The cruelest of all the old witches. An evil, jealous sorceress who had ensnared Loki with pretend appearances and false affections. But then she left him to learn the powerful ways of the darkest monster we have ever been stupid enough to call human—an old wizard whose power grew as great and terrible as the varied ways he loved to torture other men."

"Oh my." Za trembled. Talby growled even in his sleep.

"But no mind to her. No one has seen hide nor hair of her warty nose…or that cruel disgrace of a man, now that I think about it, in eons."

"Go on." Za sat back and wrapped the furs tighter about her cold feet.

Suori brought her a cup of tea with honey and sat down, a tear in his eye. "I tried to keep the witch away from your mother, but witches are known for their trickery, after all. And before too long, that old woman showered your mother with gifts and trinkets, some laced with the kinds of dark magic that only the oldest gnomes can muster."

Za took a sip and relished the new warmth the tea brought her tummy.

"I offered my hand. Wrote letters. Sent flowers. All of them returned unopened. Maybe your mother didn't want to marry me. Maybe she didn't think she could love someone as mild and meek and humble as me, but…"

"Oh my God, you really did love her." She sat her tea down and placed her warm hands in his. "Thank you for telling me."

"Yes. Baby, we all loved her. But I loved her the most. I think anyway. Now I'll never know." He squeezed her hands and then set them free.

"Go on. Please."

"None of us know what really happened next. Just that your mother was obviously with child, way too big too fast, and wouldn't leave her home. I sent more letters explaining that I would raise you as my own. That we could restore her honor. That…that I would say we had eloped, that you were mine. That the baby, or babies as it turned out, were mine. We could leave the village. Run far away. Never look back." He sniffed here and turned away. "No response. No reply. Nothing."

Za grabbed his hand again and dropped her eyes.

"And the day after you were born, she was never seen again."

"What?" She jerked back so quickly that her mug fell to the floor and shattered.

"No one ever saw her body. No one pronounced her dead. No one viewed the body to offer blessing for her journey along the Ebon Branch of Death as is our tradition. Odin simply announced she had passed on and that her memory would be seen only in the reflections of the eyes of those who loved her. A small mirror was hung from the lowest rung of the appropriate branch of the World Tree, and we were each allowed to say goodbye to her but nothing more."

"No funeral?"

"No." Here he broke down and openly cried. "And then we were asked to never speak about it again, never to say her name. The mirror was put inside the tomb for safekeeping until you four were old enough to look into it yourselves. That was… well, how old are you?"

"Eighteen."

"Eighteen years ago."

"I'm so sorry. Is this some kind of cruel joke?"

"No, I'm sorry. So sorry. That is why we, well, I at least, go silent when we see you sometimes. Because, Za, you of all the girls look the most like her." He embraced the girl he would have gladly raised as his, given the chance, and shook with emotion.

And for once, instead of pulling away from an elder's embrace, she dug into it and wished with all her might she could take it all back and make things right.

"I would have gladly been your father even without her, but how was I to care for four girls with no mother? How…while I worked all through the night, having no idea how to raise you even if I were home? Damn it." He dropped his arms, looked her straight in the eyes, and then tenderly kissed his fingers and pressed them to her cheek.

Za whimpered, and so did Talby.

"So…Odin took you in as his own, and I have been his loyal servant, in ways I am not allowed to speak about, ever since for not sending you off to some orphanage in some far away land. Even if he"—he shook his fist at the sky—"never gave me a chance to save her body, to offer her my own blood after the delivery, never allowed me to see her records and make formal accounts of the cause of her untimely and unfair death. I assume it was, as usual, infection or hemorrhage, but I'll never know for certain."

Za whimpered again. Her words failed her.

"I'll never know what really happened. God, what I wouldn't give. Nothing I wouldn't offer up. Nothing."

"And"—Za swallowed—"you never married. Is that why?"

"How could I? Any new love would always be a lesser love. Your mother was my one true love."

"Oh." Za bowed her head. She had a one true love. One she had ignored or run from for far too long. "And you have no children of your own because…"

"Well, none in the way that you think of having children. But…Snow…that is what I call your mother even in my own mind these days"—he smiled glancing off into the distance —"because I vowed never to speak her name in exchange for being the one, one day, to tell you how I fancied her. God, be good and keep us all so safe from our shadow-selves. And forgive me, Odin, for uttering such a forbidden word earlier." He dropped to his knees and whispered a quick prayer because everyone knows forbidden words are always recorded in the Akashic Record, written as scrolls on the highest leaves of the World Tree in the moments between seconds by Heimdall, the Watchman of Asgard, who always hears and notes such things with his infallible ears and perfect penmanship.

Za dropped to her knees beside the good doctor and waited until he was done. Then she helped him into his bedchamber because he was almost too weak to stand from the pain that his confession had caused him.

"And that is why I made my home here," he said as he crawled into bed. "Each night, I look out my window, hoping, praying for what exactly I can't say. I'm just too tired to…" And then he was gone with slumber as a single tear coursed down the dried up salt of the ones that came before it.

Za gathered Talby up into her arms and locked the door. With her free hand, she put the key back under the rock next to the statute of a raven, maybe fifteen centimeters tall, on the doc's porch. She grabbed the lantern next to it, more shocked that upset. "Oh, Odin, you are a monster for keeping me from knowing she was loved," she said walking down the path in front of her and shaking her fist at the sky.

But instead of turning right to go home, she turned left and went back the way she came. Back toward the crypt.

SIX

Za Finds the Harp

UNABLE TO RESIST THE PULL, Za stopped at the family tomb and entered. She located the mirror, and without looking directly into it, she took it down and held on to it like a child holds their favorite blanket for comfort. Initially, planning to quickly glance into the mirror, the same one she had ignored for way too long, she wandered to and fro to gather the courage to look directly at her reflection while she said some silly thing. But the harder she tried, the more fitting words eluded her. As silent as Odin was when she asked for advice from him, she pursed her lips and let it swing back and forth from her hand.

Had she loved her mother? Had her mother loved her? Was there some poem, some song good enough to express so many overwhelming emotions that washed over her like the tide washes over the shoreline—grief, hope, anger, fear, frustration, regret, desire, curiosity, more anger. Funny how little time she had spent thinking about her mother these past eighteen years, and now, suddenly, she couldn't seem to think about anything else. Yet here she was, as silent as a door. As mute as her adopted All-Father. As quiet as a newborn foal trembling on legs that just don't know how to hold it up.

Since talking didn't seem to be a possibility, she took to stumbling about, hoping her legs would get stronger with each step. Hoping, like the foal does, that she will run in a field of flowers instead of always falling down.

Before long, she was lost in a corner down at the end of one of the longer tunnels down the right side of the massive tomb— the space oddly and ethereally lit up by the streams of moonlight coming in the evenly spaced holes in the roof above and reflected back and forth off all the walls by a complicated maze of glass plates perfectly placed to do such a thing.

And there, she saw it. Something she had never seen before —a harp, black as death's wings.

And like the sirens call the sailors to the shore with their beautiful voices, the strings of the mesmerizing instrument claimed her, too. She touched it but once and then backed away in overwhelming fear, certain that it, like the rocky shoreline, would crush against the edge of some magical force destined to destroy her. A pool, perhaps, of eternally dismal blackness and dark matter that had existed before time or stories or gods or goodness. A harp, one that must be her mother's harp if it was here, could be no less magical than the mirror. Only it felt wrong, stolen, yet beautiful and enchanting all at the same time. She wanted to touch it and never stop. She wanted to play it and never go back home. She wanted to drop everything and become one with the melody of power it suggested. Maybe then her legs would finally hold her up for good. Or was it bad? Hold her up for bad…

Knowing that magic with that kind of pull shouldn't be taken lightly, she ran immediately from the thing back to the entry of her mother's grave. Za stared directly into the glass still hanging from her arm. "Forgive me, Mother, but I will speak your name. Nevis. Nevis. Nevis." And just to be sure the Watchman of Asgard, with his ever-reaching ears, heard her directly disobey Odin and told him so, she said it three more times.

Once outside the Crypt De' Norn, she stumbled on something over the edge of the concrete stairs and landed on her back with a large thud. Talby barked.

"I'm okay. Are you okay? Is the mirr—?" She looked at it again and swore it was not her own face she saw. She shook her head, and then her own face, more surprised and tired but the same as always, looked back at her.

Had the precious glass cracked? No, not at all.

It must have been blessed, or cursed, with powerful magic to keep it from cracking under the impact of such a violent fall. But thankfully, it was fine, and in fact, it seemed to shine like a light was coming from the back of the glass that quickly went out when she looked back at it again.

"Now I'm hallucinating. Oh, fut-a-ducks. I'm the dreamy one now," she said and laughed at her sleepy friend from the bar's favorite bad word—fut. Her old pal who had, in fact, been snoozing in the bed he loved more than life itself for probably two or more hours by this point.

Still, she couldn't shake the significance of what she had learned today. Did her sisters know? Had they lied to her too? What treachery she was victim to by the silent mouth of Odin.

Talby whimpered, and she remembered how late it had grown as she whimpered with him. "It's a long way home, Talbs. I'm glad you're always by my side. What will I do when…?"

The fox tilted his head, his ear falling forward, and he whimpered once more as if to say, please don't say it; don't even think it.

She added, "We deserve so much more than this."

Then she thought back on a few terrible things she had done. Well, more than a few terrible things. She had been busy causing bother in too many realms to mention for a long time now. "Maybe you do, at least. Maybe I deserve this. Maybe I was never good enough to be loved by my mother."

Talby shook his head and barked. He tried to tell her about the deep red apple she had tripped on, but she was too upset and fatigued to figure out his game of charades.

"Looking in the mirror one last time, Za said, "Mother, if you ever loved me, if you wanted me to find that harp, then prove it to me. I will return tomorrow to see what magic you have to reveal to me. And if you do not, then you are dead. Dead to me, I swear it, and I will shatter this mirror, no matter the spells that protect it, into so many pieces no one here on Earth or in the land of the gnomes shall be able to put it back together. Damn you for abandoning me. Damn you, Nevis, Nevis, Nevis."

And then she marched the long journey home through the outer woods, back into town, unable to escape the creepy glance of a raven that seemed to follow her every step. Despite Talby baring his teeth and barking incessantly at the bird, it managed to be close by every time she glanced up. Maybe she had imagined that like the face and light in the mirror. *How ridiculous, a bird following us. Faces. Lights. Absurd.* Maybe she had lost her sanity at the grief of knowing there was so much more to her mother's story than Odin had even so much as hinted at.

"You silent ass of a god," she whispered. "Ass god. Asgard. Hmmm, wonder who thought of that." The word play made her laugh enough to make it inside without crying. But once in the door, with the mirror still clutched in her hand, the thin but strong Norn beauty fell surprisingly easily into a deep but troubled sleep on the first night she had played the harp.

Tossing and turning, she fought evil gnomes with dark magic and ran from velvet worms and spiders as large as taverns are wide. Once if not ten times, she hollered out in terrible suffering. "Why didn't you love me? Why did you leave? Mommy! Mommy! Why did you have me if I was no good? I would have rather died inside you than live this life without you."

And somewhere, an outside observer might have described it as a bit difficult to pinpoint, yet not too far in the distance, a raven cawed back each time the black-haired youth screamed. And everywhere, an inside observer might have described it as easy to pinpoint, close…like it was right in Za's hand because it was, a white light, as white as the first few drizzles of a new winter's snow, flashed each time the pale and gorgeous young beauty hollered for her mother.

Although no one knows for sure how it happened exactly, legend to this day has it, that night that Za played the harp for the first time that anyone could remember, one branch of the World Tree seemed to change. A small but undeniable change at the farthest tip from the center of the lush and majestic green tree, where but one gnarly and terrible branch grows black as ebon night. The Ebon Branch of the Dead, for the first time in ever just at the very tip, morphed from impenetrable blackness to white—white like the first drizzles of a new winter's snow.

SEVEN

Back to the Sixth Day—Za Names the Ebon Harp

PULLING HER FINGERS QUICKLY BACK, she looked round her and wondered how much time had passed, lost so deep in thought, and turned to the next page of the manuscript that described the finding of the source of the harp via the information of a musician asked to help Sir James play it.

"Yes...it is indeed as I suspected. It is the Ebon Harp of Gnopt, fabled from antiquity as the very harp of Amoth Von, the necromancer."

Two words struck a chord deep within her—Gnopt and necromancer. She knew Gnopt as the name of a region some hundreds of miles away, rumored to have been destroyed by the evil of a sorcerer who delved into things that humans weren't meant to delve into. And necromancer was a word she didn't truly comprehend. But she knew Latin and some Greek and felt the word must, at its root, mean something close to "dead body, divination, by means of."

Words of the woman in the tavern returned once more. *"Raising the dead."* Could this Amoth Von raise the dead? Was he the dark master himself?

"Yes, but what about reclaiming the stolen?" Za asked the

silent harp. But she was used to asking unanswered questions of gods and magical things enough to let the question linger on her lips like honey lingers on the legs of a bee about to sting the one who wants to steal from it.

She moaned, drawn with an urge beyond her cognitive understanding to play the harp. Like the hands of a long-lost love, she yearned to be consumed by its seductive elixir. So she shook her bracelet, hoping that would lessen the draw, and thankfully, this time it did.

A wave of nausea shot through her, and her head pounded, her fingers burning as if some furious insect had stung her. Perhaps from effect of being so close to the harp for so long. She shuddered, horrified yet intrigued by the addictive nature of the instrument, and decided she had better read on before touching the drug-like strings again. She didn't know enough to predict what would happen next, and she didn't trust herself to stop once she started playing it. So she clasped her hands tightly on the book and hoped, like the dead hope to receive pardon and escape eternity in the underworld, that Sir James would tell her what happened to him. Maybe he could finally give her the answers no one else seemed to possess.

The book said…

"Amoth Von dwelt of old upon the Isle of Gnopt, south of the Parothian Gulf, in his high skull-shapen castle, long before the black Priests of Gnopt had ever dreamt of their accursed religion."

What religion? Za wondered. The only religion she knew of was worship of her neglectful All–Father, Odin.

The vision of the pretend barmaid making promises and dropping hints in exchange for Za playing the harp returned. She wore an old black robe around her bared shoulders that could have been soot-covered purple now that Za thought about it. A purple robe like a priestess might wear. Maybe even a priestess of Gnopt.

"For ages he dwelt there, practicing his egromancy and other arts forbidden to man, fashioning articles and objects that have no purpose on Earth but which are useful…outside…"

"Like a harp, I bet," she said and petted the small red fox that had appeared at her side from nowhere.

He barked a short and simple bark that sounded similar to a cat's meow.

"Talby, my love. You came despite your tired legs. But how did you get in?" The question should have made her take pause, but it didn't. The book was getting too good, too close to answering her questions.

"It was said," the text continued, *"that Amoth Von played upon the harp serenades and melodies no human ear was meant to hear, melodies that lulled and soothed ears other than those of men. And moreover, it was said that, played properly, the harp could…"*

"Could what, my little fox? Could finally help me find my stolen—"

Talby barked again, louder this time, and leaned back on his hind legs to make his little growl more menacing. Za laughed, and the poor thing whimpered and slumped to the ground in defeat because again she kept ignoring his warnings of peril. First the apple on the stairs that made her fall the first night she played the harp and now the open doors of the tomb that had let him in.

Still grinning at Talby's ferocious growl, Za paced round the harp, some four feet high and three feet across, and noticed for the first time that there were no turning keys to keep the instrument in tune. The word "instrument" struck her for a moment. The term meant both a tool or implement for delicate work used in pursuing an aim…a means of sort, as well as person who is exploited or made use of…a pawn, puppet, dupe.

She read a few sentences more of the book and then walked round again to see if the markings on this harp were the same as Sir James has so adequately described as markings of composers, notes of some sort.

"Surely this is a thing of magic. Thankfully, we know about magic, don't we?" Za said to Talby and became even more determined to decode the harp's true purpose. And while she read James's description of the second night he played the harp, she went back in time to the second occasion she herself had touched the piece of musical brilliance. His words were perfect to describe the feeling, almost the same words had she spoken them herself.

"With a slowness of silk robes rustling in a breeze…it seemed that with a mere stroke, the harp fairly played itself. My eyes closed like a sleeper, carried away by the music… bewitched by sweet Lorelei voices.

EIGHT

Day Two: Za Claims the Mirror and Reveals the Harp

STILL EXHAUSTED from a poor night's sleep, Za tried to get out of bed but couldn't muster the effort and pulled the covers back over her head. "Up. Up. Up," she said but didn't obey herself. "Up. Up. Up. Butt up, Za. Up now!"

Nothing. This was going to be a doozy of a morning. She yawned and closed her eyes. "For Odin's sake. Get butt up!"

Talby barked. He was up now. She should be too if only for retribution. "Bark. Bark. Bark." Za heard, *"Food. Water. Door. Ball. Pet. Play. Door. Door. Food."*

"You're probably about to pee on the floor, aren't you?"

"Bark." But Za heard, *"Yep. And I can't clean it up so… Door. Door. Door."*

She laughed. *Just the trick.* An old terrible song that her nursemaid used to sing to her in the worst possible nasal tone. "It's time to get up. It's time to get up. It's time to get up this morning." *Awful yet highly effective.* "I'm up, damn it."

With swift efficiency, she accomplished the critical tasks. Door open. Water in bowl. Food in bowl. Rushing to the bathroom herself.

Standing up, she glanced from the mirror above her small

bathroom sink down to her mother's mirror on the table before her. The reflections were similar but not exactly the same. Although she couldn't quite describe the difference, she felt more than saw the difference between her two "selves." One felt lighter, and the other felt heavier, darker, more tainted, more drained. But surely that was ridiculous. Like ravens that follow you or mirrors that flash. Pure fantasy.

She rubbed her eyes and applied some cream to the dark circles beneath them and lip balm to her cracked lips, knowing before she had even finished it was a total waste of time.

"No eye cream can cover up that, baby fox. I need a full-blown spell," she said while Talby marched back and forth between her feet on an imaginary eight-shaped track built on the love of an animal for his owner. "Oh, you stop that and lie down before your aching joints act up, little fox. Now for that spell…hmmm." Za laughed, probably because there were no spells for such critical things as dark eye circles. Thus, the entire cosmetics industry.

The red creature lay down as told but not before licking his milk bowl to make sure it was still empty. Za washed her hands and cracked her knuckles. Talby just watched. Za cracking knuckles usually meant she had a plan. A devious one.

When she cracked them again, he barked.

"Yes, I am scheming," she said, picking up her mug and finishing her coffee.

He whimpered softly, tilting his head and dropping his ear…probably hoping to convince her that sleeping in or at least staying home was the best plan of them all on Saturday mornings.

She picked up the mirror and looked deep inside her own dark eyes. "Here goes nothing. Mirror, mirror, in my hand…" She paused, unable to think of anything clever and put the mirror back down. Because for a proper spell to work…it both must be witty and rhyme, probably. She paced back and forth in the small, simple space. "What rhymes with hand?"

Talby whimpered again.

Za replied, "A fox who sleeps, makes not a peep." Probably hopeful Za would call it a morning of rest, the red beauty wagged his tail. But then she went on cracking her knuckles, so he covered his eyes with his paws. She laughed, certain she understood him perfectly. "Hand. Land. Sand. No, it's all wrong. Eyes, maybe?"

Then she dressed to distract herself from thinking too hard.

"Eyes bright." Pants on.

"Light." Undershirt.

"Hmmm." Sweater and jacket.

"In my sight. Or better yet, gravesite. Oh, that's good." Heavy winter boots on.

If a fox like Talby did such things, and he wasn't trying to sleep, he probably would have clapped.

"Okay, Talbs, re-approach. Here goes nothing but silliness. Mirror, mirror, in my…sight"—she looked directly into the glass—"take mine eyes and make them bright."

Still nothing.

She sat down on her bed, put the mirror aside, and laced the leather boots up to the top.

Talby snarled softly, rolled onto his back, and went back to sleep. Za could impress him after his nap as far as he was concerned, it seemed.

"Maybe to make this work, I have to claim it somehow. Like I the rightful owner. And maybe to claim this mirror…I have to, I don't know…name it?" She tapped her chin. "Mirror, my mirror, from mother's gravesite." She saw a quick sparkle course across the front of the glass, so she kept going. "Mirror, my mirror, from mother's gravesite, take mine eyes and make them bright."

She stared at her reflection. The circles were still there but just barely.

"Wow, I'd say that worked. Okay…putting this away." She hid the mirror in her top drawer and tried so hard not to think about the mirror that all she could think about was the mirror.

"You missed it, Talbs. Snooze, you lose." The creature whimpered in his sleep, probably chasing a rabbit. "You leave those helpless bunnies alone. Into town, I go."

Talby immediately jumped on all fours and wagged his tail. Just the word "town" cured him of all the laziness that ailed him.

"Oh, I see how things are. No, Mister Lazy Pants. No market. No bones. No pig tails. I'm going to talk to Doc. He has a clinic on Saturdays, and I have a secret to tell him." She glanced at her drawers but did not grab the precious mirror.

Talby tilted his head back the other way, most assuredly his cutest look, but even that couldn't convince her to take him. "Stay here. I'll be back. Promise."

And two quick pets later, she grabbed her bo staff and headed out the door to find the man she wished had raised her as his own.

"Strawberries yes berries. The red kind with all the dots and the green cap on top. Yes, if you can find a few…this late in the season, they will naturally pull fluid off of your feet, Widow Brokk. But haven't I told you that before? I think, ten times. Maybe I should do a memory test on you instead of a leg check today?" Doc said.

The older woman slowly adjusted her shoes, lingering longer than all the other patients. "Doc, what do you think?" she said and raised her hem a few inches.

"Totally normal."

"Normal what?"

"Your legs look totally fine to me."

"That's better. Fine, oh I like…" The woman swallowed hard.

"You like what?"

The woman growled all of a sudden. "You like…her?" The old but fair-looking woman gritted her teeth and shook her finger at Za, who approached from across the yard. "I should have known. This explains everything. Bit young, don't you think? Normal, my ass," she added, dropped her skirt, and stomped away.

"She," Doc said, pointing at the grumbling and complaining woman, "says the weirdest things. And her legs are never swollen. What a waste of my—"

"You're kidding, right?" Za laughed and twirled around for a curtsy.

"Kidding? About what?"

"She obviously fancies you. I don't blame her. I mean look at you. Tallish, handsome, sweet brown eyes. Those biceps and that cute dimple. Finish off with that flawless olive skin, smooth bald head, and lush, silvery beard… Yup. Can't blame her. Still cut at sixty." Za winked and grabbed his arm.

Doc grinned, unable to keep eye contact while he blushed just faintly enough that his cocoa-colored skin concealed it.

"You mean fifty," he said and winked back.

"Okay, fifty."

"Well, fifty-nine. For a few years now." They both laughed. "What, besides my charming and undeniably good looks, brings you round here, little lady?"

"I have…it." Za swallowed and looked at the ground. "If you want to see it."

"It?" he asked.

She dug her toe into the ground. "The mirror."

"You mean, THE MIRROR? But I assumed—"

"Ass-u-me, right? Yes. The magic mirror. You can see it, but only if...if you tell me more about"—Za sighed deeply —"about her."

"Deal. I'll tell you anything I know. But I won't say her real name, only Snow. I worried all night about being cursed for saying what I said even once. Terrible dreams."

Chills shot through her. "What dreams?"

"Nightmares about spiders and worms. Millipedes as huge as trolls are ugly, with their creepy antennae that can read your mind. Leeches that suck your blood to feed some hidden monster—"

Za stopped him by touching his hand. "Me too."

"A monster that smelled of death and rot." Doc swallowed and put his other hand on his stomach, swallowing a second, a third, a fourth time.

"Me too. God that smell. My dreams, the same." Za swallowed with him.

"Can you usually smell things in dreams?" Doc looked up, trying to smile.

"I don't know. But I did last night. The stink of a horrid, slimy monster."

Doc nodded.

Za gagged. "A creature...hidden behind drawn curtains that should never be drawn back or risk revealing the worst things that have ever been named. Things that I knew instinctually wanted to rummage through me like a wild pig does its slop. And...dark elves or gnomes or I don't know what kinds of creatures whose pointed teeth—"

"I know. I saw them too—double rows, razor sharp. The largest in the back, black as night. Ebon, even. The same color as the dead arm of the World Tree. The Ebon Branch where the damned go, trapped for all eternity."

"The only branch," Za added, "of Odin's tree that doesn't lead to Asgard."

"Yes." Doc removed his spectacles and wiped the sweat from his brow despite the wintry chill of a cold gust of air.

"Has anyone ever…?"

"Crossed back over? No." He put his glasses back on and grimaced. "That is why it is so dark, a void of any color at all."

"Exactly what I feared." She bit her lip and sighed. "What if they weren't dreams but…"

"Don't say that. Don't you ever say that. If we can see in where they are, they, those demons, my precious thing, can see out. Out here where we are."

Za covered her mouth and swallowed again. But her secret refused to stay in. "Maybe this is because I found something else. In the tomb after I left you last night. A black—"

Doc put both his hands on her shoulders. "Black. Like the branch of the tree?"

"Yes. Just like that."

He moved his hands up to her lips. "That's a bad omen. Shush. Hush. Don't say any more. Not here. Come. I know a… a place where neither Heimdall's ears nor his scrolls will discover us."

NINE

Za Follows Doc to the Cottage in the Woods

THE PAIR of them walked down a path in the woods that curved first to the right, past Doc's home, then past the crypt, just before the width of the walkway withered to almost nothing such that they had to walk behind, instead of beside, each other. The tall, red trees grew thick overhead, and the ground was littered with leaves that had piled up for too many years to count. Za swallowed, trying to remember if she had ever come this far even as a curious child.

Rabbits and deer rustled underfoot, never visible but always nearby. And as usual, a raven seemed to follow, jumping from the top of one tree or shrub to the next. Za shivered from the cold, hoping they would stop soon because her feet were getting sore and blisters wore on the back of her heels.

"If I had known, I would have worn better shoes," Za said, stopping to rub her feet.

"Hush. Keep going. They will heal. I know a tincture to cure it."

Here the ground became so covered in pine needles that Za removed her shoes and walked bare.

"Better," she said.

"Hush. Tread lightly," Doc said, and the raven cawed.

"But—"

"Hush. Ears you cannot see but that can surely hear you are always listening."

"Oh, beeswax," Za said. "I am not afraid."

"I know. That's the problem."

She stuck out her tongue and smacked him gently on the back of his shoulder with her shoe.

"Finally." Doc sighed as they approached a cottage Za had not seen before. Once inside, he sighed even deeper. "There are things—some good, some not—that are always listening to the words we speak. Words are currency of sort. Like money, we buy experiences that we purchase with those words."

"That's ridiculous." Za laughed trying to lighten her mood. How many terrible things had she said in her short life? Too many. Way too many.

"Is it? Harsh words bring a harsh life. Kind words buy a kind life. Have you not noticed that those who always complain always find more things to complain about?"

"Well…" She thought about that. "Yes. I guess that's true."

"And is the opposite not also true?"

"Well…"

"So if you are not sure what you are about to buy, then be silent. A wise man once told me that he who speaks less, often does more. So…" Doc smiled and winked, probably pleased with himself because it was his own quote after all.

Za put her finger over her mouth until they followed the cobblestone path up the front door and they were safely inside the tiny abode. The brick house, twelve meters across or fewer, had a thick thatch roof with a small smokestack above. Inside were four small rooms that seemed to encase a central closet kept tightly shut with too many locks for her to count. Around it, a kitchen sat on one side, dirty dishes piled up high, and in the small living area on the other side, classic handmade musical instruments were strewn about in the corner—a lyre, a hornpipe, and a pan flute to name a few. On the farthest side of the house was a bedchamber with seven beds lined against the wall, and a small washroom was tucked next to it.

"What's that closet for?" Za asked.

"For me to know and you to never find out. Anyway, sit and tell me what you found," Doc said and followed her to a small sofa in the living area. Quickly, he tucked a velvet, red robe into a large basket. "Never mind this. Sit. Sit. Sit. Here's a better blanket to warm you with."

Somehow, there was fresh soup boiling in a kettle next to the fireplace, and while they ate a basic fish stew from dirty bowls, she told him of getting lost in the crypt and finding the harp.

"I see," was all Doc said and chewed on his lower lip.

She set her bowl down. "So do you—?"

"Did you play it?" he asked, taking her bowl into the kitchen.

"Only once."

"Once is probably enough to crack the…" He slammed the bowl down. "Tell me everything else that happened in the tomb."

Za sighed.

"Describe your mother's grave to me. Please. Please. What did her headstone say?"

But just as she was about to tell him the grave was empty, three men marched in the house, giggling, bags tightly drawn shut to keep their contents from spilling out behind them.

"Oh, hello, Doc," Bragi said and blushed. "I didn't realize she… Well, ah shucks, Za, it's nice to see you. But why…? I mean, how…?" the shyest of the seven men from the local tavern said and looked away. "Did Odin involve her this year?"

He sat his bag down and stepped in front of it so Za couldn't make out what was inside.

Doc replied, "Nope. She's here for something else entirely. Go ahead and put that away."

Za waved her hand, and her bracelet flashed, just like it did in the crypt near the entry basin, while three men swiftly tossed their sacs into the closet and locked it back up again.

Each man returned a separate key, made of pure gold, to their back pocket and sat down to eat the fish stew.

"That, my sweet child, is a lovely piece of gold," Ull said and came over to examine her bracelet. "Is that a…? Oh my. That, my little one, is birthed from the magic of draupnir. He sneezed. "Dang if my allergies aren't bothering me again. Only in the snow and mountains do they seem to settle."

"Draupnir?" Za said.

Doc laughed. "Another day, I will explain. But the short version is that the gnome Sindri forged the original for the All-Father to gain his favor many, many years ago. Every once in a while, it splits into another. And each has a special mark upon it that tells of its unique magical property. It flashes in the presence of similar magic." Doc took a gold key from his back pocket, and her bracelet flashed again.

"Oh. Cool," Za said.

Divar, the last to finish his soup, belched.

Doc laughed. "Manners, Divar. We have a lady with us tonight, you know."

Za giggled. "That's okay. That's the most I have ever heard you say. Tell me more." She stood up, gathered the bowls, and took them into the kitchen. When she returned, Divar started moving his fingers quickly back and forth to make his special signs in the air.

"He says—" Ull started, but a sneeze stopped him.

"He says," Bragi stammered, "that…that…you are as…oh

man."

"That," Doc finished for them both, "you are as beautiful as your mother. And he is right." He turned back to Divar. "She looks so much like Snow that I can hardly look at her sometimes as well."

Divar smiled and blew Za a kiss.

"Thank you, Divar. Thank you, Doc. I am honored that you loved my mother."

Then Bragi stood up, grabbed a lyre, and began to sing a song about a beautiful maiden made of snow and angel's wings and how her handsome prince finally comes as she passes on. How the prince brings the lovely maiden both a ring of gold and his eternal kisses. How he might trade his life for her safe transport along a bridge of rainbow dreams back home. How in death they spend forever together like they had planned, but failed, in life.

One by one, the three other men joined in the song, each playing an instrument, except Divar, who simply tapped the beat of the poem out to the pleasant tinkling of a spoon and his golden key. As the song played out, they all smiled and dance and sang. Even Za twirled round the room, dancing with each man in turn to the melody so light and lovely that it couldn't be denied.

"I wrote that song down"—Bragi laughed—"for my best friend who sometimes is so damn smart that he forgets that even the most unlikely dreams do still come true. How only death might bring us the things life has denied us."

Doc coughed and stopped him. "Off to bed, you three. The Solstice is near. You need your sleep, and I have a young, and very alive I might add, lady to safely walk home."

"Thank you. I loved it," Za said and twirled one last time. "I forgot how much fun love is to dance to. I love you all."

"You know," Bragi said, "this place is a mess. If you don't

mind helping us get it…well, up to a lady's level of approval… well, we have more songs where that one came from."

Ull sneezed. "You are always welcome here. You always have been. And it is safe here when other places are not. Magic makes this place hard to find."

Za remembered that she had never seen the house before. "Oh, now I see."

"But before, you didn't. Now you do," Ull added and wiped his nose.

Divar smiled with his cheeks and even bigger with his bright blue eyes. He brought his fingers and thumb together and touched his cheek at the side of his mouth. Then he moved his hand closer to his ear and touched his cheek again. With his lips, he mouthed the word "home."

"Home. Lovely. I understand. Thank you. I do feel welcome here." Za grabbed her bo staff and wrapped a blanket around her shoulders. "Talby will love it too. So many scraps on the floor." And they all laughed.

Doc took her home, holding her hand and telling her all his stories about her mother along the way. The way her mother was more afraid of spiders than anything else but was still too kind to kill them and would carry them, her worst enemy, outside to avoid hurting them. How her mother had a slight green sparkle in her eye that drove the boys crazy. How her mother loved the scent of skunks and danced when she thought no one was looking. How her mother's voice was so beautiful but, since she got easily embarrassed, never sang in front of anyone but him. How they met three times before they realized they had already met. How hummingbirds would let her mother hold them. How children she didn't know would raise their arms to her, hoping she would carry them. How you could look into her deep brown eyes and see the center of heaven.

Before long, they passed the crypt.

"And now, she's in there, and I'm out here still missing her. Cruel joke, don't you think?" He swallowed and frowned.

"No, she isn't. She isn't in there," Za said and sighed.

"What? But that's impossible." Doc dropped the stick he carried. "Don't—"

"I've been trying to tell you. She's not in there. Her mirror was."

"Was? What? Of course she is," Doc said and stopped walking, the grief coursing across his face like the lyrics of the saddest song ever written.

"No. Her grave is empty," Za said and gasped for air, the breath knocked out of her by what she thought it meant. "It was all a lie. A trick. A ruse."

"No!" He leaned into Za, not sure if he was holding her up or she was holding him up.

"What else could that possibly mean?"

"Now that is a question worth asking, Za. Grave robbers, maybe?"

"Couldn't get in. Not without this." She raised her bracelet.

"Body taken somewhere else by Odin."

"Unlikely. Why bother? He never bothers."

"You should give the All-Father more credit than you do, little one. One day, you will see. But why isn't she? When? How? I would have noticed it if…"

"I don't know. I have no idea. I didn't even know you knew her until yesterday."

"True. Oh my God, Za. What if she…? What if she is still alive? Take me to the harp. Take me now. Take me now, Za!"

And so she did, and together, they played it for the second time. Doc looked on while she played the harp to the same melody of her mother's song from earlier. And if that had been lovely, this time the tune was too magnificent for words to describe on the earthly plane.

TEN

The Sixth Day—Za Continues the Collected Written Works of Sir James

RETURNING from the memory of four nights prior, the night she played the harp for the second time after telling Doc that her mother's grave was empty, Za sighed and shook her head. So much had happened in such a short period of time. If only she knew back then what she knew now, she would have done things differently. She would have moved the harp before playing it the first time. She would have never played the harp.

That was a lie.

Nothing could have stopped her from playing the harp. It was her only chance to get her mother back. If the woman she had seen really was her mother. She had to know more. Maybe she could still move it? She knew just the place if they would let her. Of course they would. Maybe that's why she had seen the cottage.

In the distance, a raven cawed, and she took that as a sign. She liked signs; they had a way of pointing things out that fate had already determined needed to happen next.

Besides, the abundance of coincidences in Sir James's text up to this point no longer shocked her. She was a fate after all, and destiny was destiny. Za realized she had no choice but to read every word of the precious book now. Her very destiny depended on it. Like maybe he had written it so that it could save her. Maybe it hadn't saved him. Maybe she still had a chance and thus, her mother with her.

And so she read on...

"The following day, I busied myself with such researches as were possible into the history of the harp."

"Finally some good news, Talby. Looks like James had discovered what I could not about its original owner."

"...his early exploits and accomplishments such as building his house with the aid of inhuman hands and succeeding in the shunned arts of necromancy..."

That word again made her swallow hard, and the light in the tomb flickered in and out just enough to let her see that the snake had indeed caught the mouse.

"Who is the mouse here, my tender and aged friend?" Za asked Talby, who simply rolled over in his sleep and whimpered softly. "Who is the snake?"

And she read on for another hour or so before she had to take pause and eat a few bites of her salty bread to calm the growing pit in her stomach. Whether she was more hungry or afraid, she had lost the ability to tell. Until she came to the next part...and knew it was fear, not hunger, that made her eat.

"A history which, for the benefit of those whose eyes may gaze upon this manuscript, I repeat here.

"The harp of Gnopt shapen in dubious realms by the joined efforts of the Sorcerer Amoth Von and **Those who are not to be named,** *who dwell in spheres outside the earth and realms uncounted and unseen by men."*

Za tried to figure how the harp could be here if it was such a terrible and forbidden thing of darkness. Had her mother known of such arts? Was that why she had died, or pretended to die?

Was that why the tomb was empty? And why hadn't she seen the harp before this past week or so?

Surely Odin had been in here. Surely he would have banished such a device of power and torture in direct opposition to the religion of worshipping him. Then she remembered the hand plate at the gate. Surely *None Potest Intrare Norns—Only Norns May Enter*—did not apply to all-powerful, higher gods like Odin. Or maybe there was some ultimate power in this realm, more important than even Odin…her adoptive father. But if that were the case, then had the black harp been here all along? Hidden maybe. Recently unearthed? Why? How? By whom? As the thoughts consumed her, the lights flickered four times. *Four times… Interesting.*

Za counted the Norns she knew—four, her three sisters and her.

Her fingers went up—one, two, three, four. She crinkled her nose, and in a high-pitched singing voice, she recited the legend of the Norn Sisters as she had read it some time, or was it tyme, ago.

"Once upon a time, there was born a quartet of intriguing girls, each an incarnation of destiny and life itself, with very special yet potentially deadly gifts. And as the four sisters had no mother and no father to speak of"—here she grunted twice before continuing in a normal pitch—"and were innately able to wield such powerful magic, they were placed directly under the guardianship of Odin—master of their Universe." (Few more coughs and grunts.) "He called them Sisters of the Norn and placed them in the greater service of the good of his domain, which he ruled in a fair but oft' misunderstood way."

"No kidding. Misunderstood is one way of putting it," she said to Talby.

The red fox would have rolled his eyes if a creature like him could do such things. Instead, he barked. Well, almost barked. It is hard to know what sound a fox makes after all. "What does a fox say?" Za giggled and thought of an old song that used to make her laugh. Talby barked three more times to be clear.

She continued, cooing as much as mocking now that he had forgotten to be afraid of what Sir James had written.

"Determined to mold the Norns' natural gifts in a positive manner, Odin assigned them each an honorable task with respect to time. The first and most beautiful (pointing finger in the back of her mouth and gagging) sister, Urtha, was made responsible for managing memories of the past. The second and most charming (dip, curtsy, dip), Vertha, was made responsible for the present moment. And the third, the most creative (sticking her tongue out) of the quartet, Skulda, was made responsible for the future. But the youngest, a spirited and often distracted creature named Za…that's me, foxy fox…refused to be made responsible for anything as complicated as time."

Talby tucked his tail. "So, so, so, so very true. Let us continue…"

"And thus to keep her…I mean, me…out of the way of the other three, Odin assigned her the simple task of wasting time.

"And so while her sisters served humanity under Odin's guidance, Za played and dreamed and played some more."

The words sounded more glamorous than her life felt. But she was here with the harp, and none of the others were. All three of them surely busy doing this or that for some stupid mortal. Maybe she should be more thankful for how much Odin left her to her own devices now that she thought it through. If he were always around, he would probably be around just for bossing her around, not helping her out. Best she helped herself then.

Odin had given her few pieces of advice that had ever helped her now that she considered it. In fact, the most useful thing he had told her was to speak to her mother's mirror. When

Za had asked him why, his answer was that mothers had ways, even from the other side of their graves, to help their daughters. *What mothers? What daughters? There are none here. Only orphans.*

A single tear trickled down her cheek, which she quickly wiped away before the fox saw it and got any ideas about her wanting the mother she never had.

"Fiddle-fut-a-stick and spinning tops on that." Za sniffed and returned her attention to the crumbling book in her hands. "For fox's sake, we have a book to finish, and it's getting later by the minute. Where is that Doc when I need him?"

On she read…

"Many are the gates and doors thereunto, and many are the realms whereto drifts the music of the harp. The idiot flute players join in the melody, and even Cthulhu does hear the strains. And even as the door swings both ways, and the seas wash to and fro, so shall the gates. The music shall grant entry to other realms or open the way unto this time and the sphere for the entry of them who choose.

"The door swings both ways. I knew it, Talby. I knew it. And the music, oh…"

She stood up, stretched her arms, and rolled her neck, hoping Doc or one of the others would arrive before she got much further. She was close to the end now. She needed him now more than ever. What had happened?

On she read…

"Bubbling Azathoth held no terror for Amoth Von, and the gulfs of Kyath no fear. And in the end, the thaumaturge sought out those far beyond the Red Star and Yuggoth's hidden locale. And did shun even Yog Sothoth, who is the gate, but sought out his own passageways. And he penetrated realms of which even Cthulhu has heard, but dimly, and has known in the midst of his nightmares.

"Yea, Amoth Von called, and sought beckoned even unto them which no words can describe, nor mind can bear. And in the end, he did succeed in calling one of them, as legends avow. And what that one did to the Sorcerer is beyond the power of the human mind to contain."

And much like Sir James himself said, Za too was both disgusted and drawn to the words she read. Unable to put it down, she continued to read despite the fading hours, which had for the first time ever…found a way to escape her hold on it. It had gotten late. Almost too late yet on she read…

*"Many are the ways and varied the means of traversing the spaces even unto special elixirs and incantations and rituals that affect the opening of temporal gates. And moreover, there are instruments, playthings, and mechanisms known to the Elder gods and those **outside**. And there are ways to open the portals that no man may know. And there is the harp.*

*"And few are those of mankind who know the enchantment of the notes and the lure of the tones. But they that do shall have all things revealed. Even unto the forms of **them** who wait at the most hidden on gates and secret of the realms, even unto the face of **him** which lurks behind the spheres."*

Za remembered the monster from her dreams or visions. The same that Doc had suffered with her. A creature that smelled of death and rot, hidden behind drawn curtains that should never be drawn back or risked revealing the worst things that have ever been named. Things that she instantly knew instinctually wanted to rummage through her body like she was food to feed its evil intentions and nothing more.

She read on for a while longer and learned that after many years, the Sorcerer Amoth Von seemed to disappear, and even his Black Priests and Priestesses violated his castle to find the harp. Even they, who offered human sacrifice and performed the most terrible deeds, loathed the power of the harp and used every possible mechanism, physical or magical, to destroy it. After finally giving up, they locked it shut with golden chains and a golden lock, forged from the gnomes themselves, and tossed it into the watery abyss around the Isle of Gnopt.

Here Sir James described being drawn to play the harp where he played it for the third time. Where he saw a vast expanse and a woman who walked around in a beautiful blood-red dress in a perpetual mist. The text described her gossamer dress and her creamy shoulders. A raven's blackness for her hair. A soft hint of a tune she hummed as if waiting for only one person who knew what the song was about. The description, uncanny and perfectly worded, reminded her of someone. Someone who, although she had always wanted to, she had never been properly introduced to.

Za closed her eyes and remembered exactly what the woman looked like when she saw her the third time she played the harp as well.

ELEVEN

Za Plays the Harp for the Third, Fourth, and Fifth Time

AFTER ONE TIME through the undeniable melody, Doc pulled Za's hands back and stared at the awesome instrument. The sheer power of it reverberated through the air alongside with the song it played, hinting at what this might mean.

"It might…" Doc started.

"I don't like might," Za added. "We need facts. We need more time to be sure."

"Promise me that you won't touch it while you are alone."

"Pinkie promise," Za said and wound her little finger tightly round his like a small child saved from danger hugs their heroic parent.

"Good. Thank you. If you…" Doc looked away and cleared his throat. "Just don't. Don't you."

Za wiggled both her little fingers. "Double pinkie promise."

"Well, there is no doubt this is powerful magic. Whether good or bad intending things put it here, I cannot say. But I do know your mother was always a being of light. And the darkest things oft cling to the lightest things, hoping that if their gods have forsaken them, maybe, maybe they can find another way back home from what they have done. If not, for their levels of evil, they will suffer that many rounds of pain in the Under-world. The shadow world, where only pain remains."

"Do you think everything…even the worst, most terrible things want to be good?"

"Who am I to say? Only Odin knows. But I hope. I do hope."

"Me too."

And so they went separate ways that night, and each alone suffered even more dismal dreams in dark and painful places before the morning light of the following day.

As soon as the sun came up, Za came round Doc's door knocking. But he was nowhere to be found. Not at home. Not at the clinic. Not at the tavern. In fact, none of the seven were at the tavern. A *Closed, Be Back Soon, Joyful Solstice Wishes to You* sign hung on the door.

Za tried to remember the last time the pub was closed and realized it had been maybe a year or more ago. No, she realized. It had been exactly a year. She had gone looking for a last-minute Solstice gift for Talby and found the sign on the door. Same last year. Exactly the same.

So she went back to the crypt and did just what she had promised not to. Talby barking the whole time, she found herself sitting in front of the harp, unable to not play it.

"Some promises must be broken for other promises to be kept," she whispered, certain of and also completely confused by what she had just said. Somehow, she knew that advice was more for her to hear than say.

Talby groaned and sat on her feet, probably to keep them warm.

And as a tune flowed from her fingers lightly touching the strings, one she had now heard for the third time, this was what she saw. A vast and misty expanse floated in and out of her vision. In amongst this space between shadowy constructions, a beautiful, forlorn maiden in a red gossamer dress seemed to hover atop missing feet. A raven, or at least some black, similarly shaped bird, floated back and forth, whispering in the woman's ear who said nothing but only hummed a tune in perfect timing with the very same one that Za somehow inherently knew how to play on the strings of the Ebon Harp.

Za sang some of the words she remembered from Bragi's song before.

"One sure fine day, my love will come.

One sure fine day, he will find a way."

She missed a few lines here and then dropped back in.

"I had a dream the other night,

That we only die once.

And when my time comes,

He will be the one to bring me home,

To castles of old that I've always known.

One sure fine night, my love will take me.

One sure fine night, I'll be his bride.

The death bells will ring for us,

And his, I'll forever be…"

A few more lines she forgot at this point before finishing the song.

"When that sure fine day comes,

When I finally die in his arms."

Za watched for some matter of minutes that lasted less than seconds and longer than forever all at the same time. And just when the woman took notice of her singing the song and turned round, the vision faded. Both the realm and the girl instantly gone, and the harp grew silent but not before Za saw a glimmer of color from the maiden's eye. A faint but undeniable flash of green from the side of her sad, deep eyes.

That night, the third time she had played the harp, Za's sleep was even more troubled than before. Only this time, her visions were plagued with horrific and torn images of the woman in place of the monsters. The woman weeping uncontrollably. Her tattered red dress ripped to pieces by cruel winds that must have come from evil frost giants trying to punish her for unspeakable crimes. The raven, once her familiar, pecking out her eyes in retribution. A shattered and crumbling bridge she must cross, but can't, to survive the bloody waves that crashed on the shore to suck her under a sea of liquid, metallic death. Devices of torture no good man ever had a need for. Metal, knives, and hooks holding the woman down, piercing her mouth, removing her breasts, amputating her legs, excising her skin and leaving only rancid flesh beneath. Her body left to fester in the scent of rot in place of the perfume she should have worn instead. The terrible stench itself, the prime source of all misery that ever existed in the darkest of unspeakable places still infected with evil too terrible to survive. Babies abandoned in cribs, bees and beetles circling round their eyes. The woman's chest bursting open and where the heart should have been, a black pit of dismal pus. A man on top of the woman, taking things no man had any right to without consent over and over and over again, leaving the woman's womb filled with velvet worms and leeches. As a result, insects as large and ugly as trolls that tore her apart from the inside as they birthed from what was once her sacred divine center. Now left empty and godless, her eyes gone, replaced with pieces of shattered glass that cannot see images but only reflect shadows of what was once possible and then taken away.

To say Za didn't sleep was an understatement. Each time she tried to fall back into slumber, she trembled in fear that her next dream segment would be worse than the last. Eventually, too afraid to try again, she got up and made coffee instead. A burning hot bath helped for her to think she might compose herself enough to go find Doc and tell him what had just happened.

But again, he was nowhere to be found.

The more she searched for him, the greater her need grew to find and save the woman. Was this woman her mother? Was she some witch trying to trick Za? Was this some side effect of the evil power that oozes from the harp? Who, other than Odin, could say? And Za was not about to go ask him, her neglectful ruler. Never around. Never helping. Never guiding. So many nevers.

So again she went to visit her mother's crypt, mirror in her hand, looking for answers that do not exist on Earth or in Asgard or even Gimlé. Gimlé, the highest heaven above Asgard where one immortal god was rumored to rule the other mortal gods below. Gods that must answer to someone else, gods like her All-Father, Odin. And while the several notes she left for Doc and the others at the tavern went unanswered…she tried to rest; she tried to ignore the harp but couldn't.

So on that next day, desperate for answers no matter how dark and terrible, she plucked the strings for the fourth time. Only music played. No visions. No other realms. Nothing other than a few flickers of light from her bracelet and even darker eyes looking back at her from the beautiful mirror.

She tried again. Despite playing it a fifth time, nothing came but music.

So home she went, and for too many hours for her to count, she slept soundly, like the dead do in Hel's arms in the Underworld, with her faithful Talby standing guard at her side until once again she awoke.

When Za finally opened her eyes, Doc was there. How he got in, no one could really say.

"The chimney, of course," he replied when she asked. And although they both laughed, she didn't believe him. Not at the time anyway.

"Some secret powder lets you down. That's funny."

"Nope. No powder. A bracelet, maybe though," Doc said, and Za's bracelet twinkled in response to the magic to which Doc alluded. They both laughed again, she because her friend was so silly and Doc because he was totally serious.

"We must move the harp," she said. "It isn't...safe." She sat up and yawned.

"No, it's not. And you shouldn't have played it without me. Not once. But twice. Oh, Za, you crazy thing," Doc said, bringing over warm mittens for her hands, followed by a nice cup of hot chocolate. He drew the curtains back and let the sun in.

"The firewood. Out back, there are..." She rubbed her eyes. "Wait. How do you know? I didn't tell you. Start the fire, and I'll explain over breakfast."

"Nope, not a chance, Za. You are coming with me. I'll feed foxy while you dress. Bring layers. We have no idea what to expect when we get there."

"To expect? Where?"

"Damn, you pinkie promised. Are even pinkies no longer sacred?" He grinned, but she felt his fear, his concern underneath his kind expression. The kind of disappointment a father might hide under the joy of knowing his child was okay after a long trip away from home.

"I'm going to get it later, aren't I?" She put her hands on her hips.

Now he really laughed. "Yep. Expect lumps of coal. But not from me. I told you Heimdall was listening. He hears everything. He knows when you are awake. When you sleep. When you break promises. When you keep them. He sees it all, writes it all down on a permanent list."

"On the leaves of the World Tree. Yes, supposedly." She coughed.

"Not supposedly. I've seen the lists. I use them to decide... Anyway, they are always accurate. I read what happened when I got back from my other job last night. Where are your shoes, Za? Why haven't you put them out?"

"Shoes? For the Solstice Saints? I don't believe in that old crap shot legend. You must be kidding."

"Nope. And they believe in you whether or not you believe in them. I assure you that when something is real, your faith in its realness is a moot point."

"Hogwash! Total crap." She downed her coffee. "Wait. What other job?"

"It's an old story. Anyway, gather yourself up. And put the shoes out. That's a doctor's order, lady. Not a request. Things just got real."

"Real?"

"The Ebon Branch of the World Tree is changing. I think the harp is involved. A higher power, the highest actually, has sent me to help you...navigate this."

"Wait, what? Changing? How?"

"The tip of the branch has turned from a void of blackness to a pure color of white...like snow. Like snow. Do you hear me? Do you understand what I am saying?"

"I opened a portal into the... Well, the harp did."

"She's there. I'm sure of it. Tell me what you saw, and I will help you find Snow. I mean Nevis. I will help you find Nevis."

"But you vowed not to say her real name."

"None of that matters anymore. What is done is already done. There is no going back for either of us now. I found her. I found the one who is to blame for all of this to begin with. She will pay. Pay dearly."

"Who?"

"The ogress. That bitch. She's coming for the harp. She thinks we can play it. I told her we could show her how. She's coming to claim it. So tell me what you know before she kills me for not knowing it." He leaned in to hug her, and she let him.

"I'm sorry," Za said and swallowed.

"I know. Before I forget, take these two things. They are all I have left of your mother. Her hair ribbon and her hair comb. As long as I have these, that creature won't have all of her. Because once he does...once he does, everything changes, and his power is complete."

She looked at the two items—a small, simple, bone-colored hair comb and a ribbon, also small and simple and lovely. "They are magical, yes?"

"More magical than you know. I think, and I could be wrong, that before she left you, the pain of being torn from you left part of her soul here in these. Odin gave them to me and said never to reveal them until it became obvious your mother's power of pure love was necessary to save you. Maybe even save us all."

Za pursed her lips, unable to speak.

"That time," Doc said, nodding at the items, "is now. Tell me what happened."

"I played the harp. I did. I saw her only once. Mother, I mean. I think it was she anyway. Red dress. Raven on her shoulder. Marble skin. Pouted lips. Deep, sad, worn down...no, drowning eyes. The next two times I played it there was nothing but music. But that song. The same song you sang at the cottage. It's like I know it. Like it knows me. I know the lyrics but shouldn't. I can play the tune without trying."

"I figured no less. Like you've heard it in your dreams."

"Yes, like that." From across the room, she saw the mirror flicker, and even though she might have imagined it, it felt like the comb and ribbon moved slightly in the direction of the mirror. Like they wanted it. "Tell me about the song."

"How about we let your mother tell you…when we find her."

And so they left and went back to the crypt for the last time that Doc ever would. For in a short while, everything would change. Why? Because the door had been opened from impossible to possible, and now this solitary possible path of destiny had to be played out. For now, there were no others.

TWELVE

Za Tries to Move the Harp, and Angerboda Returns

DOC LEADING THE WAY, Za following closely behind, they reached the Crypt De' Norn about mid-day.

They had stopped to check out the World Tree on the way. Doc had been right. There was no denying the white edge of the Branch of the Dead.

"What does it mean?" Za asked, gasping at the subtle but shocking change.

"Well, it might mean many things." Doc swung his bag onto his back and straightened his shoulders. "None of them seem very good. Might be really bad."

"Might—my favorite word. Thanks." Talby ran ahead to chase a rabbit but came back when Za called his name.

"Good boy," she said and petted him, letting Doc approach the large receding doors first. Oddly, they were slightly cracked. Talby growled and ran over to the doors.

"Weird. Let me help." Za put her bracelet over both their hands together, filled the red bowl, and the doors opened wide enough for them to enter. As they stepped over the threshold, a snake or maybe a large worm of some sort slithered back out. "Double weird." She shook her head and tried to ignore the chills down her spine. "You were saying…about the tree. White. Meaning…"

"Oh, yes. But no one knows for sure. It's never looked that way before. We have to keep moving swiftly. I'm not sure how we will move the harp to a safer place. I called the other men, and they can help but not until after sundown. They are still collecting the last of the…" Doc paused. "Za, what is your greatest wish? If you hung one from the tree, what would it be?"

"To have my mother's things. And now I do. A mirror. These two items. So, I guess my wish was already granted this year." She smiled and brought the delicate ribbon to her nose, inhaling deeply.

"Our wishes are always granted, darling. Sometimes we just can't see it. Until later. Until it becomes clear. You know, some of the greatest gifts come in the most unusual of ways. The more you believe, the faster they can come to you."

He put his hand on his belly and laughed, hard and deep.

"When I see it, I believe," Za said and stuck her tongue out.

"Nope. When you believe it, my love, you finally see it."

"Whatever." She laughed but then looked at the crypt. "I sure do love to hate that place."

Doc laughed and nodded his head, seemingly feeling the same way. "Let's do this thing and get ready for the boys. Tell me more, Za."

"Creepy. I don't want to be in there after sundown again." She thought about the worm that had escaped. "Well, if you must know, the last things in my dreams after playing the harp suggest that the monster is torturing that poor woman and making her stay. I think he…does things to her. Terrible things."

"I think," Doc said, cleaning his glasses and looking the other way, "that we have to consider the possibility that you are right. And that the monster is something much more horrible than a monster. Remember what I said about the ogress, Angerboda, who left Loki for an even darker master? Well, what if…?"

"Let's not go there yet. Let's get the harp to the cottage. Okay, I'll take the mirror now and try to think of a spell powerful enough to lift it." She wandered back and forth saying a few words for several minutes.

"Mirror, hmmm nothing. Maybe…lift, sift. Remove, soothe. Carry, fairy. Dang this will be tough."

Doc grinned waiting for her to be done. Za was a terrible spell caster, hardly a witch at all, it turned out, and that made him happier than he had been in a while.

"What are you doing? Stop listening. It's embarrassing. Get the mirror, Doc." She groaned, blushing.

"You brought it, not me. Where is it? I'll grab it. Maybe in here."

He fumbled through his bag but stopped when he saw the look on her face. "Oh no. It's still at your place. Dang. Dang."

"Well, trying never hurt even if we are destined to lose, I suppose. You never know when impossible will become possible," Za said and sized up the harp.

She walked around twice before stopping long enough to put her hands across the top.

"You hold it steady while I lift from below." Doc, completely bent at the waist, heaved, but nothing moved.

"Oh, bend your knees. You're a doctor, aren't you? Even kids know that."

Doc smirked but did as told. "I'll count to three, and then we try again" He steadied himself. "One. Two. Three." His face turned red, and gas boomed out his backside, but the harp never even faltered.

Za was about to thump the strings in anger, but Doc grabbed her hand just in time. "Not yet. Not yet."

"Wow," Za said. "Thank you." Then she sat down and groaned while Doc walked around it. He pushed here and there, but nothing seemed to work. It was like the harp had fused with the floor and become part of the crypt itself.

"Too heavy. Or maybe too stubborn. Magical things have a way of showing their personalities. And this thing is a right demon," Doc said, wiping his brow with the back of his forearm. So he took some golden chains out of his bag and locked it up tight.

"What, exactly, are you protecting it from, Doc? Ain't no one going to steal it."

He laughed. "I am making sure it knows who is boss."

"Sure," Za said. "I'll get the mirror then, Mister Bossy Pants."

"Good, and I'll gather the boys. We can meet back at the Dvergr's Tavern and after dinner, make it a group effort. Keep the other two items safe."

"Okay," she said, hurrying back out. If she had known she would never see him again in the land of the living, she would have hugged him tightly. Probably would have cried even. But she didn't know. Neither did he.

But the snake, a velvet worm to be exact, from the corner knew. And when both Doc and Za had left, she turned herself back into an ogress and laughed, picking up the remains of the deep red apples she had used to poison the other Norn Sisters to get into the crypt in the first place.

"Fools. I have all of you now in my grasp. All of you. Ebon Harp, I will have you next. Mirror, you too, my beautiful glass. And Amoth, my immortal beloved, you terrible creep, I will finally make you pay for loving Nevis more than you ever loved me. Even though I did things for you she could never do. Why? Why?"

She shook her hands to the heavens.

"Odin, mark my curse. You are not the only one who knows how the tree lives. Loki told me in his sleep that the Sisters Norn and their basin of swirling liquid waters your precious tree with never-ending life. And without the immortal sisters to nourish it, all the branches will change bit by bit. And as the balance between the nine realms you have so carefully established falls, so falls the world as you light and lovely Aesir Gods created it. And we will go back to a better time. A time when there was no earth, no sun, no moon, no stars…only Niflheim, a waste of frozen fog above, and Muselheim, a place of eternal fire below. But in between these two realms, for untold ages that existed before the concept of time or light, there was a gaping pit of dismal and dark energy. And after the concept of time and light, so it shall return, and those that worship it shall reign over all the world in misery once more."

THIRTEEN

The Dwarves Fall Prey and Za Seeks the Book

BACK AT HER SMALL QUARTERS, Za gathered the mirror and looked deeply into the alabaster glass. But what she saw was not her own reflection. It was her mother's.

"Mother, it is you, is it not?" Za wiggled her nose up and down, but the reflection didn't change. "Yes, I thought so. I'm listening."

The woman in a red, tattered dress looked back at Za intently through the glass. "Hush. Be quiet, or *he* will hear us," she said in the slightest voice Za had ever heard. Then she wiggled her nose side to side to confirm that Za was not hallucinating.

Za almost laughed. But then she remembered her dreams—the pain, the suffering, the violation. "He is the monster. He holds you against your will. He did…things to you."

"Yes. So much worse than a monster. But for all he has taken from me…he has also given me the only things that matter to me anymore."

"Explain yourself."

"Hush. Baby girl, ask the witch about the book. It is too late to explain more right now, but you are in grave danger.

The entire tree is trembling on this side. We don't have time for this. Or tyme. There is simply no more left to waste now."

Za grabbed her bo staff and readied herself. Her own reflection returned, but she could hear the woman behind the glass humming a tune—the tune of a prince who comes for his bride in death.

She whispered in between verses. "The only thing *he* allows me is this song. As long as I give myself, my body, to him, he allows me this one thing. He thinks the song is about *him.* So I sing it. He knows there are two pieces of me he doesn't own yet. He's obsessed with owning me. He thinks owning me means loving me. He thinks the key is the two missing verses. But it is not."

"The comb and ribbon," Za said as a fact, not as a question while she held them tightly and put them back in her pocket. Then she remembered that loving someone was more about setting them free than owning them.

"The song is all I have to keep him from consuming all of me. I sing, acting like I am trying to remember the last few lines. But that's not true. I know them all."

"So do I." Za nodded and placed her hands in prayer position over her chest.

"Yes, but once he has the other two things, he will have all of my light and love. My love for you. Once he has that, the balance here will shift, the Ebon Branch will fall, and I can never find my way home to Asgard where I can watch you from above, not from inside, behind, and beneath like I watch you from the shadow world." Another tear fell. "It's all I have ever wished for."

"So as long as the ribbon and comb are here, you suffer but…" Za swallowed.

"But I get to keep a connection to you. My sight of you in

the mirror. It is how I have watched you grow up. Other than you in the glass, I have no reason to go on."

"And so Odin said to visit the crypt to speak into the mirror. It was for you. He wanted that for you. Not for me. Oh, Mother, I'm so sorry I failed you for so long." Now a tear dripped down her face too. One. Two. Three.

"Hush. Dry it up. He will feel your suffering and come even faster. And suffering never helped anyone. Sadness is okay, but suffering is the ultimate waste of life. The ultimate disgrace to the life that called you forth." Nevis cleared her head and straightened her shoulders. She could bear her torture one more time. She could always take the pain one more time while she held out for the hope that one day her true prince would come. He would find a way. She was sure of that like she was sure of her love for her daughters and the goodness of Odin, her god.

A terrible stench filled the room. "He's coming to find you," Za said. Her mother nodded. She shook her head and wiped away a tear.

"Yes. Listen carefully to words hidden inside the verses." And so the song began again. Only this time, Za heard the song inside the song. For in every fairytale, no matter how light or dark, there was always a song hidden inside a song. Just like there was always a story hidden inside a story.

"One sure fine day, my love will come.
  Find the book by Wizard James.
  One sure fine day, he will find a way.
  Move the harp.
  I had a dream the other night,
  I will help you no matter the cost.
  That we only die once.
  She already has the seven men.

And when my time comes,
He will be the one to bring me home,
To castles of old that I've always known.
But you must pretend you do not know.
One sure fine night, my love will take me.
One sure fine night, I'll be his bride.
The death bells will ring for us,
And his, I'll forever be…
Go. Go to the tavern and meet the witch.
When that sure fine day comes,
When I finally die in his arms."

The mirror went dark, and the crypt filled with a silence so loud it burned her ears, the sound of silence unbearable to her now. The song forever burned on her brain, Za arrived at the Dvergr's Tavern.

When an old woman opened the door, Za acted like it was nothing unusual.

"Oh, hello," the maid said, going back behind the bar. She looked twenty at most. Blond hair, large breasts, inadequate clothes for the season for sure. The disguise didn't fool Za like it had obviously fooled Loki, the greatest trickster of all.

"You are new," Za said. "Where are Vestri and the others?"

"Well," the young thing said, "maybe those guys are the Solstice Saints and I am here as their ultimate relief of sorts. Drink? Stew? Apple pie? The boys loved my apple pie." She pulled her black blanket up around her shoulders like a shawl.

"I bet. But I'm allergic to apples. And I don't believe in the Saints."

"Oh, pity that. Drink then?" The witch laughed, trying hard to lighten her cackle into a usual sort of laugh.

"No. I don't drink. I'm looking for Doc. Have you seen him?" Za smiled.

"Nope. Don't know him. Is he a regular here?" The maid ran a dirty, old cloth across the rim of the glass, leaving it even dirtier than it started.

"Sort of. He's the dark handsome one." Za winked.

"Oh," the witch said, looking up to the left and smiling. "Yes, he is. I mean, nope. Neither hide nor hair from him. Whoever he is."

"He's bald, charming, quite clever. Lovely beard, too." Za sat down and put her elbows on the bar like she owned the place.

"Yes. I mean…oh, okay. I'll keep an eye out for him." The maid bent over, swished her black apron to the side, and took a pie out of the oven without a mitt to protect her hand. "Pity you won't have some. This was made just for you."

"Made for me? Odd, considering you had no idea I was coming. Doesn't that burn?" Za asked.

Immediately, the maid set the pie down. "Of course it does. Old, I mean, slow nerves. I hardly notice the heat." She laughed and then clenched her teeth. "Sure you can't have one little bite?"

Za scratched her cheek. "So if ever I was…yep, sure." She cleared her throat and crossed her legs. "I'm here," she said, "hoping to talk to the bald hottie about a book by a Wizard named James and about a harp. An Ebon Harp, to be exact."

The young woman gasped. "Never met him. James or the hottie." She was getting frustrated now. The drinks and apples weren't working. She needed a new plan. A new way in.

"Are you sure?"

The witch smiled. "Well, maybe. Maybe. Let me think about that."

"Good. Think about that then," Za said and checked her fingernails while she twirled the barstool around a few times.

"You're not much of a reader, surely...are you, dear?" The barmaid twirled the glass in her hand as though it were a miniature version of Za on the stool.

"No, not much. That's true," Za replied.

A satisfied glance went across the woman's face. "Good. That's good," the wretch had added, and Za was immediately reminded of a few of the stories she liked to whisper in the ears of those terribly stupid brothers Grimm. *Good? Not good.*

"But I like a nice story," Za told the woman. "In fact, I am always on the lookout for the next tale. Where are you from anyway?"

"Gnopt."

"Funny, Gnopt funny," Za teased but thought better of it. "I mean, funny. I've never heard of Gnopt."

"Ah, that might be true, child with such a lonely heart, but we in Gnopt have heard of you."

"Me? How odd." Za stood up, grabbed her bo staff, and put it across her body like a weapon she intended to use.

"You are...how shall we say...quite infamous for what happened with the releasing of the Enfield creature. Lovely staff. Know how to use it? Show me."

"Of course." Za twirled it around her body, fast and tight—five, six, seven times—and slammed it down on the bar right in front of the witch. "That is how it's done. But the Enfield was not a creature, he was a..."

They talked for a little while longer, the staff strategically placed between them, both playing the other but getting nowhere. And when Talby growled at the young woman and tried to bite her, Za said, "Best to be leaving then. I'm sure we shall meet again."

And sure she was, and so was the witch.

While Za rushed back to find the book, the ogress turned back into her terrible self—long, gray hair, split up the ends, knobby knees that held her up over oversized feet that had never fit in a ladies' pair of slippers. Her hands, withered and terrible, could have been centuries old…because they were. Deep purple robes hung to the floor, dropping spiders and leeches as she stepped.

She went in the back room of the tavern and force-fed all the sleeping men rotten apple pie, filled with beetles and velvet worms, until they were no longer sleeping but almost dead, their guts rotting from the inside. Dead enough for their souls to begin to take the first steps of their journey down the Ebon Branch. Dead enough to be served up as food to the largest velvet worm of them all by his loyal servant even after he had forsaken her.

And while the witch decided which was best to burn down first, the tavern or the World Tree, Za searched for and found the infamous book. And as quickly as Heimdall's ears hear all broken or kept promises, she returned to the crypt.

It is here that we rejoin our story back from the beginning as Za returns to present time.

FOURTEEN

Za Returns to Present Time and Moves the Harp

ZA CLOSED THE BOOK. She couldn't take much more. She had read enough for now. The final page could wait. Time was just too short.

Sir James's descriptions swirled in her mind. The forbidden yet alluring harp. The woman he saw, obviously Za's mother named Nevis. The wizard's warnings gathered speed to her fears while the song of Doc's love for her mother embraced and soothed them. She simply had to move the harp and see if, she were to cross into the shadow world, she could save her mother. Could she save her seven friends? Could she thwart the plans of Angerboda, who obviously wanted to use the harp for dark and terrible purposes? So many questions. So many. Too many.

Could she even move the Ebon Harp? Did she have enough power?

She removed her bracelet and put it around the base of the mirror, hoping the combination would be more effective.

"Mirror, my mirror, from mother's gravesite, take this harp and make it light." The room brightened, and the harp seemed to glow. "Give it wings like angels' fair. Make the harp fly and take it there. There to the cottage of Snow's love so true. Take it, take it, take it, take it through."

Sure it would work because it was her best spell ever, she grinned. But then she stopped. The light went out, and the harp turned back to normal.

Then she remembered the book. Sir James had played the harp for a sixth time. One in which he almost entered, but didn't quite completely step into, the shadow realm. Maybe she could do the same.

She sat down to play and took a deep breath. The timing couldn't have been more perfect if Odin had willed it himself. Then she realized maybe he had.

"You old bugger," she wailed at the sky. "Damn you for being here even though...you are not. Nevis, Nevis, Nevis," she added to make sure Heimdall heard her and wrote it down on his ridiculous naughty vs. nice scrolls.

Lightly touching the strings, the lyrics of her mother's song seemed to float across the ceiling, through the air, and over her like a magical blanket. But oddly enough, new and different words came out of her mouth. Bits and pieces of new lines guided as if by some unseen higher power. The words were these:

"Play the Ebon Harp with fingers light...
    Wait, dare not to touch, lest you might,
    Bring such demons forth...this Solstice night.
    Unless...unless...
    Your blood-red kisses of life, do trade,
    Otherworldly passion of love's fairest maid,
    And you're the only creature who ever stayed.
    Safely abreast the devil's malicious shore...
    And by helping Snow be as black as noir,

Forever closed an un-closable door.
The harp shall go.
I, the All-Mightiest of the All-Mighty, will it so."

And in a flash, Za, Talby, and the harp all arrived at the magical cottage in the woods whilst outside a raven cawed to warn them that a stranger approached. She barely had time to stand before the first knock came.

FIFTEEN

The Witch Reveals the Truth

ZA PEERED OUT DISCREETLY, but the young barmaid spotted her. It was no use pretending. Za opened the door enough to expose the chain. Talby growled, ready to bite the woman.

"What do you want?" Za pulled her bo staff up to her face so it could be easily seen.

"The harp. That is all. Give me the harp, and I will leave you and the wolf alone. If you don't, I'll kill you both and take it anyway. Easy decision, really." The witch laughed a deep and sinister laugh.

The chain exploded, and the door flew open.

Za held her ground, the staff between her and the woman. "Fox, you mean. And I doubt that." She knew enough after reading the book that her odds of defeating this woman, obviously a Priestess of Gnopt, with her spotty spells were pathetic at best. She would have to kick her ass the old-fashioned way. She widened her feet and centered her weight to attack.

Angerboda laughed. "I'm not going to fight you. Not like that."

Za swirled the staff around her head and slammed it down on the floor. Bam.

"That is one cool trick." The witch reached out to touch the staff, but Za twirled it quickly enough to pull it back, spin around, knock the kettle off its hook by the fireplace, and toss it between them.

"You were saying…"

"I was about to ask," the woman said, kicking the kettle to the side of the room against the brick wall, "what sound does a fox make anyway? A wolf barks, but a fox, hmmm. Does it bark or meow or what?"

Talby barked, snarled, and had to be held back to keep from biting her.

But the woman just laughed again. "Oh, they bark. Cute. Good to know."

"Fut off, you," Za cursed while the witch cackled and raised her wand to cast her counterattack. "I want my friends back."

"Not possible. Too dead. Dead. Seven dead. Tainted with a black spell that will trap them in the shadow realm, unable to make it home to Asgard. I think," the witch added while glancing around the small, adorable space, "that I'll keep the cottage after I kill you, too." She lifted her wand even higher and raised her eyebrow.

"Wait," Za said. "Don't. Have you ever played the harp? I have. I have seen him, the monster…I mean, the man you seek. Amoth Von. I know the melody of the only tune he is willing to hear. The only song that opens the gate unto him and his darkness. I can bring you to him." Za fingered the two items in her pocket while an idea brewed beneath her bargain. An idea birthed from the mind of grace.

"You lie. Like your mother. Lying bitches, both of you. She stole my lover with her green eyes—bewitching eyes that kept him obsessed with her instead of me. So alluring she conceived several children at once. And to think, your mother always pretending to not be a witch when she was the ultimate witch in bed."

The idea grew stronger. Could it work? Chills coursed through her in an answer of sorts. A confirmation that it just might. Might—not such a bad word at a time like this.

"And now you with your seven lovers. You whore." The woman stepped towards Za, jealousy searing her face like the flames of the damned sear their souls.

Za suddenly remembered that love has little to do with jealousy and everything to do with absence of jealousy in total trust and acceptance. "What are you talking about? My mother never loved that Dark Master. She never would have agreed to be his beloved. She loved Doc." The memories of Za's tortured dreams from the other night returned once more. Her mother being sliced apart, being taken against her will, her heart replaced with black misery. "Oh my God." Za dropped to her knees from the heaviness of it. "I surrender to the truth."

"You have no god, Za. You are a liar who deserves to burn."

"Yes. Yes, that's true. I don't deserve this life. But not the way I thought." She thought of all the love she had been shown in life but couldn't see until right now. She remembered Doc's words. *Our wishes are always granted, darling. Sometimes we just can't see it. Until later. Until it becomes clear. You know, some of the greatest gifts come in the most unusual of ways. The more you believe, the faster they can come to you.* "I believe," Za said, "that I am truly loved. I am truly guided. That I can make all the wrongs right again. I will burn if that is what it takes."

The witch shook her head. "Fool. Only wrongs remain here. And if Amoth wasn't your father, I would have ripped all four of you into pieces for your evil lies. Your immortality is no match for someone like me. But just in case he wants you for some reason. Maybe he can use your sempiternal blood to feed and strengthen himself."

"My what? He's my what?" Za looked up from the floor, heaving, her hand over her mouth.

The witch thumped herself on the forehead. "Oh, don't tell me you didn't realize. The magic that runs through your veins didn't come from your mortal tramp of a mother. It is all his. All his darkness. All his power. The Dark Master's."

Za looked at her hands, at her bracelet. Shame washed through her like an evil acid rain, and she doubted like sinners doubt they can ever be forgiven their worst, most terrible crimes. She felt light, soothing pressure on her shoulder and regained her composure. Again she said the words. "I believe that I am truly loved. I am truly guided. That I can make all the wrongs right again. I will burn if that is what it takes." She stood and squared her shoulders, ready for whatever might happen next.

"Odin took pity on you, fool. You should have been banished to the Underworld like the rest of the dark creatures the moment you were born. So your kind and precious and holy mother took your eternal place in damnation for you. Duh."

"What?" She wavered on her feet and put her hands out for balance.

"The branches of the World Tree must balance, or it will fall over. Everything must have its place and position. Your mother serves not one but four sentences in the Underworld of shadows to pay that debt. Your innate debt by being born like you are—a creature of darkness born into a world of Aesir light."

Za's visions returned. Her mother in unspeakable pain. Parts removed. Raped by terrible creatures, ripped apart from the inside over and over again in penance for unspeakable crimes she had never once committed. Za stumbled backward. Immediately, she realized that every promise a mother could keep for her child, in the most unbearable of ways, had been suffered by her mother.

"Tough cards they dealt you, no?" The witch grinned. "Well, your mother at least."

Za recalled her own words from before. *Some promises must be broken for other promises to be kept.* "Oh! Mother, forgive me for every time I cursed you." Za shook, all her failures dripping off her skin and soaking the floor like dirty water that is too rancid to wash dishes and can only ruin them instead. But she refused to give in to the wrongs if somehow she could make them right. She glanced at the mirror on the table beside her and saw horrific things. Fields burning. The tavern ablaze. Children running. Women screaming. The World Tree turning white as the disease spread from the Ebon Branch to the center. Her reserve doubled, tripled until it was undefeatable.

"And that, what did you call him, bald hottie bartered for your quality of life here on Earth. He has been in servitude to Odin ever since. Taking gifts around in red sacs. Filling shoes. All of it to save you, you selfish twat who is so damn clueless that you don't believe in the Solstice Saints, while all they do, they do for you."

The idea, one that must have come from a higher place that she knew not how to name…maybe from the highest highs of Gimlé even, grew stronger still. She had to convince the witch she was too broken to fight back. "I want to kill myself. Kill me, please." Again she fingered the items in her pocket and thought of Doc's words. "*More magical than you know. I think, and I could be wrong, that before she left you, the pain of being torn from you left part of her soul here in these. Odin gave them to me and said never to reveal them until it became obvious your mother's power of pure love was necessary to save you. Maybe even save us all.*"

"Gladly. Your kill will help me achieve my twelfth level of

evildoing today. But damn, then I can't play the harp. You can play it, you idiot, because he made it and you are his daughter. Foolish girl. Crap, I need you more than I realized."

Za stood, pretending to be too numb to notice Talby wagging his tail and swirling her feet, and went to the kitchen, hopefully looking like she was trying to find a knife to slice her own wrists.

She remembered one more thing her mother had said, something about the tree trembling in the shadow realm, and the idea got stronger still. If she opened the gate fully for this evil woman, the entire tree might fall out of balance and crumble to the ground. The world of the Aesir Gods might literally unravel. And as usual, it would all be her fault.

Talby whimpered, but still she didn't turn to soothe him to make her pain seem so complete and authentic that she could never escape it. But she had to repay all the favors given unto to her and honor her mother who had suffered unnamable things for her daughters. All her mother's suffering…eighteen years of suffering. Doc's suffering. All of it. All of it for naught if she wasn't able to pull this off.

And just like the spell earlier, the idea consumed her mind, or perhaps her heart, from a place of pure unconditional love. "Agapé," Za said. "That's the word for unconditional love. The way my mother…" Za choked on the words. "I mean, the way you love Amoth."

Pride flashed across the witch's face, and Za noticed immediately that love and pride were two very different things. "Yes. Yes, that's right."

"Then I can help you. I know his favorite song, remember? I will teach you the words that will open the gate, and you may enter to claim him with unconditional love. He is old and blind now. He will think you are my mother. And when he comes to take you, you can show him who you really are. He will be so pleased, so impressed, that he will forget my mother for all eternity and want only you."

The witch put her wand down. "And I can bring him back here?"

"Maybe. I guess. I mean, yes. And together, you shall have"—Za thought about the need for balance—"a perfect swap. One witch, worthy of the suffering of seven, a mother of four, and one to spare." She set the staff down and stepped toward the woman, her arms open and light. Talby looked up at his owner and cocked his head, probably confused by the sudden change in her mannerisms.

"The harp and our power back and…" The witch smiled, obviously pleased with the plan. "The gate stays open for how long?"

Za held her fingers up—both hands and then two in the shape of a V again. "Twelve. Ummm, long enough," Za said, counting the men and her mother and making sure that twelve fair and balanced swaps would get them all out. Or across.

Angerboda scowled. "You're sure of this."

"Well, the whole town is burning, so what do you have to lose?" Za said. "Easy decision, really." They both laughed at the irony.

"True. Burning to the ground. You have twelve minutes. Go."

"Yes, take a seat, and hold the strings like this. Repeat after me. Say the words lightly. Say them softly, or he will not think you are the one for him." One more finishing part of the idea shot through her heart like a knife, and she repressed a tear. "Here. Take these." Za took the comb and ribbon from her pocket.

"What are they?"

"The things," Za replied, "that will bring him to you the fastest. So you can find him before the twelve minutes are up.

Oh, one more thing. Change your hair to black. Change it now."

And the witch did as she was told, satisfaction and anticipation spreading across her face like Cholera spreads in army camps.

"They were my mother's. He will smell her on you and not realize what has happen until it is…too late."

And as she clipped her most prize possessions in her worst enemy's hair, pretending to dress her like an adoring child helps her mother dress for a party, Za thought about Doc's words one last time. "*More magical than you know. I think, and I could be wrong, that before she left you, the pain of being torn from you left part of her soul here in these. Odin gave them to me and said never to reveal them until it became obvious your mother's power of pure love was necessary to save you. Maybe even save us all.*"

Then she touched the strings for the very last time she ever would.

Za Plays the Harp for the Seventh Time

As Za played, she whispered the words for Angerboda to sing.

And in a moment trapped infinitely between seconds, she looked round the cottage to see a mirror flash, a bracelet twinkle, and the faintest outline of a one-eyed giant, her mother's raven atop his shoulder, in the farthest corner. And across his golden face—as pure as Odin's because it was Odin's—was not the look of pride but agapé as Za repeated these words one more time.

"One sure fine day, my love will come.
    One sure fine day, he will find a way.
    For he is always watching.
    For he is always near.
    I had a dream the other night,
    That we only die once.
    And when my time comes,
    He will be the one to bring me home
    To castles of old that I've always known.
    One sure fine night, my love will take me.
    One sure fine night, I'll be his bride.

The death bells will ring for us,
And his, I'll forever be…
Because he was always mine,
And I always was always his.
It was a promise we made,
The day Gimlé's God made our souls.
When we split from one,
But appeared to be two.
When that sure fine day comes,
When I finally die in his arms,
And he in mine."

And although no one but Odin really knows how it happened, this was what occurred. The evil witch transformed into a beautiful maiden, clad in a tattered, red dress. Amoth Von came and claimed his eternal bride as his own to consume in mutual wickedness. The trembling World Tree stood still while the Ebon Branch fell off, and its balance was restored. And a harp disappeared. The Ebon Harp, to be exact.

Only the book of Sir James remained.

But the best, most wonderful thing of all, nine of the most beautiful souls to ever cross it stood high atop a rainbow bridge. Six men dressed in the same funny red suits, one man carrying a maiden in a gossamer gown, and a wizard—probably a wizard named James—all of them laughing like old pals at the tavern as they walked across a colorful, shimmering bridge. A bridge so bright and fine with fire in the color red amongst it that burns the feet of frost giants. A bridge that leads straight to Asgard. And although it had never happened before, and will never happen again, this time, it led from the falling Ebon Branch of the Dead, straight home to the castle in the sky known to all that are blessed enough to know it as…Asgard.

Nevis turned around, Doc holding her in his arms, and

waved at their daughter. After all, he had almost become her other parent. In everyone's mind, now he had.

Za tried to speak but couldn't. But that was okay. She had a mirror, and mirrors work just fine in Asgard. And she had her blessed dreams. She had them, too. She had lost the comb and ribbon. But some gifts must be lost so that others can be claimed. And immediately, Za realized that love was about the gifts and never the losses.

And as Za's first tear of joy fell, so did the first flurries of snow. Snow, pure like Nevis' soul. Snow, pure like a mother's unconditional love. Snow, pure like the heart of the Solstice Saints who had always been real whether people believed in them or not. Snow, pure like the love of a favorite fox. Snow, pure like the forgiveness of sins committed out of ignorance that are so easily forgotten. Snow, pure like agapé. Snow that can put out any old fires lit by witches so easily cast aside that no one can even recall their name.

Afterword

So on the morn of winter Solstice, Za got up earlier than she should have. Her three sisters were with her, still recovering from food poisoning. Probably from rotten apples. She went out back to get some fresh water. And that was when she saw him —Heimdall, on the neighbor's roof, trying to climb down the chimney but stuck…too fat round the middle to fit.

Laughing, Za climbed up to help free him. "That is how you get in. Oh, Doc wasn't kidding. I guess now it's your job to deliver the wishes since the seven saints are..."

"Busy partying as heroes in Asgard. Yes, that's safe to say." Heimdall grinned, his smile too big for his face just like his belly was too big for the chimney. "They call you a hero too, you know," he said and smiled even bigger although that seemed hardly possible. But sometimes the impossible was possible after all.

"That's ridiculous. Why?" Za giggled and offered out her hand.

"If it weren't for you, Za… Well, let's just say you do more than you realize."

"Like what?" She squatted down, trying to figure out how to get him out.

"You really don't know, do you?" Heimdall rolled his eyes and shifted his position, trying to get out.

"Nope."

"You water the World Tree. At the red basin by the crypt. That's what you are doing when you fill the bowl of life." He grabbed her hand and pulled up. Nothing.

"Absurd. The bowl of life. Whatever. Let's push you down," Za said and laughed at his condition.

"You are the spell that feeds the tree, little one. You." He grinned.

"Oh, guess it's not a waste of my power after all. Thank you, All-Father."

"He loves you more than you know. Whether he says it or not."

"Starting to see that." Za sat down and looked round the roof for ideas. Her bracelet flashed, and she giggled, certain it was a sign from above.

"Good. Hey, let me borrow that bracelet."

"Deal. But I want collateral. Put a wreath or something on my door."

"Done."

She handed him the bracelet, but somehow another one appeared to replace it. "Odin said I couldn't remove it. Guess he was serious. But it seems like I can pay it forward. Also nice." She took a breath and let the love of the All-Father embrace her. He did, as it turned out, always seem to have her best interest in mind.

"How did you get this gig?" Za asked.

"Well, someone had to do it, and I already had recording the naught-nice lists down pat, so I volunteered. It gets lonely up on that bridge."

"So…you were the perfect choice. Great. I'll spread the message you are real."

"Tell the Grimms and all the kids."

"Any requests?" Za grinned.

Heimdall laughed. "Yes. Great idea. Cookies and milk. And no one can see me, something like that. Something mysterious to keep the kids guessing."

"Okay. That's awesome. Done." Za bit her lip and thought about a few other nice ideas. Maybe foxes or reindeers. Maybe twelve days of celebrating. Maybe a new name like Saint but slightly different. And lights, lights everywhere. Something cool like that.

And as Heimdall disappeared into the chimney, the first Christmas as we know it today was born from the story inside another story.

But Za had one last story to weave before she opened the two wishes Heimdall had brought for her and the one he had brought for Talby.

She found that silly pair of goons named Grimm drunk as skunks at the local bar and whispered in their ears. "You will love this one. It's called Nevis. No…it's called Snow. Snow White and the Seven." She paused. "It's called Snow White and the Seven Dvergrs, which means dwarves, you know. And the dvergrs' personalities were all unique. " Here she almost cried but held it in. "One was happy, another always mad, and one so, so sleepy. One shy and bashful, one mute but never dopey, one always sneezing…and Doc. His name was Doc, the most gallant and lovely of them all. And there was a terrible witch." Here she paused to flip the story upside down and make it more clever. "The witch uses a comb and a ribbon to trick Snow White, but the prince saves her anyway. And they all die…I mean, live. Oh, how they live happily ever after."

What she didn't add was that Snow was her mother, and she

and Doc were finally together in a better place now. And although that feisty young thing will deny it to this day, when no one is listening, she hums a tune. She acts like she has forgotten the words, but that's ridiculous. One day, she will have a daughter. And one day, she will give that daughter the two gifts Heimdall gave her this year. And when she puts that precious ribbon and an alabaster comb in her daughter's hair, she will sing her a song. The song that makes a mirror light up. A song that goes like this:

"One sure fine day, my love will come.
   One sure fine day, he will find a way.
   For he is always watching.
   For he is always near.
   I had a dream the other night,
   That we only die once.
   And when my time comes,
   He will be the one to bring me home,
   To castles of old that I've always known.
   One sure fine night, my love will take me.
   One sure fine night, I'll be his bride.
   The death bells will ring for us,
   And his, I'll forever be…
   Because he was always mine,
   And I always was always his.
   It was a promise we made,
   The day Gimlé's God made our souls.
   When we split from one,
   But appeared to be two.
   When that sure fine day comes,
   When I finally die in his arms,
   And he in mine."

And sure as that one fine day will come, Odin will be watching from a corner not too far away, with a face plastered in agapé. And since he has a new familiar now, a raven to be exact, he will be able to see things he couldn't have seen with only one eye. Why? Because one eye will never do when you could have three.

Books in the Norn Novella Series

Where Tyndra Turns to Ardnyt
Where Ebon Sounds Like Ivory

About the Author

A. Nicky Hjort is originally from the greater Dallas-Fort Worth area of Texas. She writes stories that cross multiple genre lines, from paranormal romance to Sci-Fi thrillers and back again. And in some subtle way, all of her manuscripts are connected, with their purpose to explore all facets of love and what it has to teach us. Her journey into writing began with her clinical background as a medical doctor when she wrote her first fictional short story about medicine. She hasn't stopped writing since.

Facebook author page:
https://www.facebook.com/Author.A.N.Hjort
Twitter: @A_NickyHjort
Website: www.anickyhjortbooks.com
Blog: www.ANickyHjortBooks.com
Instagram: https://www.instagram.com/nickyhjort

Also by A. NICKY HJORT

Other Works by Nicky Hjort

https://www.amazon.com/A.-Nicky-Hjort/e/B01M30LVVM/

A Sinister Bouquet: Awakening Book 1: Devyn Mitchell has a choice… listen to the voice of her unborn baby – or die- again. After a near death experience, Doctor Devyn Mitchell finds herself not only mysteriously pregnant but able to communicate with her fetus. She has two choices: give in to total madness or surrender to her new reality, which just may be the only way she and her family will survive the obsessions of the Homeless Hunter's mind. A true paranormal romantic thriller, A Sinister Bouquet: Awakening, the first of the Sinister Series, will take you right to the edge of what you know to be possible and then drop you in a place so dark, so terrifying, that the only passageway out is through the blinding light of awakening. Wake up. Open your eyes. Finally. We've missed you so. (MA18+ for graphic sexual and violent content)

A Sinister Vision: Know This Much is True – Book 2: Elise Phillips, a doctor in training, has successfully repressed her kidnapping five years prior. The only problem is...she has six and one-half days to remember every terrible detail, or a total stranger will die. But to make matters even worse, in order to save this nameless woman, Elise will have to face something that scares her even more than death–intimacy. Another paranormal romantic thriller, A Sinister Vision: Know This Much is True, the second of the Sinister Series, will take you even further over the edge of what you know to be possible and guide you right back out through the only way left...impossible. Wake up. Open your eyes. Accept your assignment.... The problem is not to find the answer–but to face it. Know this much is true.

(MA18+ for graphic sexual and violent content)

Where Tyndra Turns to Ardnyt – The Norn Novellas: In the center of a magical world there grows a beautiful and terrible chasm of climbing plants. On one side of the Ivy Wall we find the hell-of-Tyndra, on the other, the heaven-of-Ardnyt. But legend has it that in the middle…lives a preternatural beast that imprisons and tortures the children from both sides. When the war against time begins, Azza will have to cross over the Ivy Wall, something that has never been done before by a living being. But if she does make it through, she just might discover who she really is and how she became trapped in this alternate reality. A fairytale at heart, this is the first chapter in the epic saga of the youngest and most fickle of the four Norn Sisters. The same feisty immortal creature who must escape her inherent inner darkness to learn the meaning of love. A veritable palindrome from start to finish, the narrative of Where Tyndra Turns to Ardnyt journeys through duality to discover what shocking truths emerge when up becomes down, life becomes death, suffering becomes release, and the most unexpected endings become the most surprising beginnings. Welcome to a place where forwards and backwards are exactly the same direction. Here Where Tyndra Turns to Ardnyt.

The City: The Jane Harvest: Winning battles means Ink honors, prestige, and life itself. …Yet nobody understands what losing truly means. On another planet two hundred years in the future, twenty-one-year-old Isla Jane struggles helplessly to figure out who she is and what her world really means. Marked with a forbidden tattoo of the rising sun, she is a natural champion of humanity and a gifted warrior in Heats– lavish battles fought in the conjoined minds of the participants for the morbid amusement of the masses. Despite Isla's desire to fade into the background, she emerges as an obvious leader of her people when the senseless assassination of a youth forces her to face the truth. Her volatile world, disguised by its elaborate battles and constant mayhem, is a prison without bars and a coffin, the lid already half-closed, that they must escape. But when she vows to find a way to bring her people back home, Isla will have to deconstruct consciousness and the very nature of the space time continuum to unravel good from evil, truth from lies, and survival from true love. Welcome to the City–where it takes lives to save lives…

Also from the Lavish family

Irrevocable Series
Samantha Jacobey
http://myBook.to/TheIrrevocableSeries

The end of the world is coming, or so they say, and that puts Bailey Dewitt on a crash course with Armageddon. Orphaned, she and her young brothers find themselves living with their renegade uncle as part of a group of survivalists. She struggles against them, searching for a way to escape, but every discovery only terrifies her more.

For Caleb Cross, the Ranch is a way of life. The members of their group are family, and none should come between them. Smitten from the moment he met Bailey, his choices are no longer easy, his path no longer clear. He wants to welcome her and the twins into their fold and hopes his kin will agree.

But the elders who lead them aren't interested in the trouble-some girl. They are plotting for the time they will be rid of her and expect Caleb to go along with their plans - he is after all one of them.

At first, Bailey resists Caleb's charms, but soon must admit that she desperately needs a friend. She has no intention of anything more, but when the elders make their move, she is forced to trust him with her very life.

They both have hard lessons to learn. Relationships built on secrets and lies don't come with guarantees. When the world falls apart around them, some things are Irrevocable.

Rosinanti Series

Kevin J. Kessler

http://myBook.to/RosinantiSeries

The Rosinanti Dragons are no more. Since their extinction nearly one thousand years ago these primal powerhouses have fallen into the obscurity of history's forgotten lore. In that time, humans have come to dominate the world of Terra, peacefully ignorant to one horrifying truth: ancient evil stirs around them, waiting to reclaim its lost world.

For Valentean Burai, animus warrior of the kingdom of Kackritta, the details surrounding humanity's victory over the Rosinanti are more than just a history lesson. The long-buried mysteries of this archaic conflict may hold the answers that he has so desperately sought regarding his own past.

As the awful truth of the Rosinanti's supposed demise comes to light, Valentean must stand together with Seraphina, a magically gifted princess, to embark upon a mission to maintain order and light throughout Terra. Only together can these two lifelong friends face down the resurgence of the Rosinanti legacy and combat the greatest threat their world has ever known.